PENGUIN BOOKS

A CERTAIN SMILE

Françoise Sagan was born in 1935. Her father is a prosperous Paris industrialist whose family were originally Spanish. She took her *nom de plume* from the Princesse de Sagan of Marcel Proust. She was eighteen years old when she wrote her best-selling *Bonjour Tristesse*. She had failed to pass her examinations at the Sorbonne and she decided to write a novel. The book received great acclaim in France, where in 1959 it sold 850,000 copies, and also abroad. Her second and third books, *A Certain Smile* and *Those Without Shadows*, have also had tremendous popularity in France, Great Britain, and the U.S.A. Her fourth book, *Aimez-vous Brahms . . .* appeared in 1959. In 1961 she published *Wonderful Clouds* and since then has published *La Chamade* (1965), *The Heart-Keeper* (1968), and *Sunlight On Cold Water* (1971). All these books have been published in Penguins. Her ballet *The Broken Date* has been produced in Paris and London. Her most recent works are *Un piano dans l'herbe*, a play (1970), *Zaphorie*, a play (1973), *Scars on the Soul* (1974) and *Lost Profile*, a novel (1976).

Also available in Penguins:

AIMEZ-VOUS BRAHMS...
BONJOUR TRISTESSE
THOSE WITHOUT SHADOWS

Not for sale in the U.S.A. or Canada

A CERTAIN SMILE

Françoise Sagan

TRANSLATED BY
IRENE ASH

PENGUIN BOOKS

Penguin Books Ltd, Harmondsworth, Middlesex, England
Penguin Books, 625 Madison Avenue, New York, New York 10022, U.S.A.
Penguin Books Australia Ltd, Ringwood, Victoria, Australia
Penguin Books Canada Ltd, 41 Steelcase Road West, Markham, Ontario, Canada
Penguin Books (N.Z.) Ltd, 182–190 Wairau Road, Auckland 10, New Zealand

—

Un Certain Sourire first published 1956
This translation first published by John Murray 1956
Published in Penguin Books 1960
Reprinted 1961, 1964, 1966, 1969, 1971, 1973, 1975, 1977

—

This translation copyright © John Murray, 1956

—

Made and printed in Great Britain by
Cox & Wyman Ltd,
London, Reading and Fakenham
Set in Monotype Garamond

À FLORENCE MALRAUX

PART ONE

L'amour c'est ce qui se passe
entre deux personnes
qui s'aiment

ROGER VAILLAND

I

WE had spent the afternoon in a café in the Rue Saint-Jacques, a spring afternoon like any other. I was slightly bored, and walked up and down between the juke-box and the window, while Bertrand talked about Spire's lecture. I was leaning on the machine, watching the record rising slowly, almost gently, like a proffered cheek, to its slanting position against the sapphire, when, for no apparent reason, I was overcome by a feeling of intense happiness, a sudden realization that some day I would die, that my hand would no longer touch that chromium rim, nor would the sun shine in my eyes.

I turned towards Bertrand; when he saw me smile he got up. He could not bear me to be happy without him. My joys were to be limited to the short and most important moments of our life together. In a vague way I already knew this, but that day I could not tolerate it, and turned back to the machine. The piano was playing the theme of 'Lone and Sweet' and the clarinet took it up. Every note of the tune was familiar.

I had met Bertrand the previous year during the examinations. We had passed an agonizing week side by side before I left to spend the summer with my parents. The last evening he kissed me, then came his letters. Casual at first; after that the tone changed. I followed their progress with a certain emotion, so that when he wrote: 'It sounds a ridiculous declaration, but I think I'm in love with you,' I was able to answer in the same vein without lying: 'Your declaration is ridiculous, but I love you too.' My reply came to me quite naturally, or rather, like an echo.

My parents' property on the River Yonne offered few distractions. I would go down to the river-bank, look for a moment at the weeds floating yellow and undulating on the surface, then choose little flattened stones to send skimming over the water like black, darting swallows. All that summer I repeated to myself the name Bertrand, and thought of the future. In a certain way it appealed to me to begin a love affair by correspondence.

Bertrand now came up behind me. He offered me my glass and when I turned round I found him close to me. He was always annoyed when I was inattentive during those interminable discussions he had with his friends. I was rather fond of reading, but literary talk bored me. He could not get accustomed to this.

'You always put on the same tune; though, mind you, I quite like it,' he said.

He lowered his voice on the last words which reminded me that we were together the first time we heard the record. I always noticed his little sentimental allusions to various landmarks in our relationship which I had quite forgotten. 'He means nothing to me,' I thought; 'he bores me, I'm indifferent to all this, I am nothing, nothing, absolutely nothing!' And the same absurd feeling of elation got hold of me.

'I have to go and see my uncle, the great traveller,' said Bertrand. 'Coming?'

He went out and I followed. I did not know his uncle and did not want to. But there was something in me that seemed destined to follow the well-shaved neck of a young man, always letting myself be led along unresistingly, except for the icy little thoughts that swam through my mind like fish. I felt a certain affection for him just then. As we walked along the boulevard our feet kept time like our bodies at night. He held my hand. We were slim and pleasing, like people in a picture.

All along the boulevard and on the platform of the bus taking us to his uncle I went on feeling very fond of Bertrand. I was pushed against him by the surge of people. He laughed and put a protecting arm round me. I leaned against his jacket by the curve of his shoulder, that masculine shoulder so comfortable for my head. I inhaled his perfume which I knew well, and it moved me. He had been my only lover. It was through him I had learnt to know my own body. It is always through the body of another that one discovers one's own, at first with suspicion and then with gratitude.

Bertrand talked about his uncle; he did not seem to care much for him. He made fun of his travels, for Bertrand spent his time looking for a reason to ridicule others, to such an extent that he lived in constant fear that one day he might unknowingly appear ridiculous himself. The fact that this struck me as absurd made him furious.

Bertrand's uncle was waiting for him on the terrace of a café. When I caught sight of him I remarked to Bertrand that he didn't look at all bad. As we came near he got up.

'Luc,' said Bertrand, 'I've brought a friend. Dominique, this is my Uncle Luc, the famous traveller.'

I was agreeably surprised, and thought: 'He looks

quite passable.' He had grey eyes and a tired, almost sad expression. In a way he was handsome.

'How did the last journey go off?' said Bertrand.

'Very badly. I had to wind up a tedious legal affair in Boston. There were tiresome little lawyers in every corner. An awful bore. And you?'

'Our exam is in two months,' said Bertrand.

He had emphasized 'our'. This was the conjugal aspect of the Sorbonne; one spoke of examinations as one would of babies. Bertrand's uncle turned to me:

'Do you pass exams too?'

'Yes,' I answered vaguely. I was always rather ashamed of my modest activities.

'I've run out of cigarettes,' said Bertrand.

I watched him as he got up. His walk was quick and supple. Whenever I thought that this combination of muscles, reflexes, and olive skin belonged to me, it always seemed an astonishing gift.

'What do you do apart from exams?' asked Bertrand's uncle.

'Nothing,' I said; 'well, nothing much.'

I raised my hand as if to suggest futility. He caught it in mid-air and I looked at him surprised. The thought flashed through my mind: 'He's attractive, he's rather old, but he attracts me.' He laid my hand on the table, smiling:

'Your fingers are all ink-stained, it's a good sign. You'll pass your exams and be a brilliant lawyer, although you don't appear to be very talkative ...'

We both laughed. I told myself that I must make a friend of him.

But already Bertrand was coming back. Luc was talking to him but I did not listen. Luc had a slow way of speaking and large hands. I thought: 'He's just the type who tries to seduce young girls like me.' I determined to be on my guard, but still I could not help feeling a pang of disappointment when he invited us to lunch two days later, but with his wife.

2

BEFORE we had lunch at Luc's I passed two rather dull days. What did I really do with myself? I worked half-heartedly for an examination that would not lead very far, basked in the sun, and accepted Bertrand's love; for though I was fond of him I did not give him much in return. It seemed to me that mutual confidence, affection, and esteem were not to be despised, and I seldom thought about passion. After all, most people appear to live without very deep emotions. One must make the most of what life offers, and that, I found, was difficult enough.

I lived in a sort of family pension, only occupied by students. The management was not strict, and I could easily stay out until one or two o'clock in the morning. My room had a low ceiling, and was large and completely bare, as I had soon dropped my original plan to redecorate it. I asked only that my surroundings should be unobtrusive. The house had a provincial atmosphere which I liked very much. My window faced a courtyard bounded by a low wall over which one caught glimpses of the Paris sky, carved into pathetic triangles above the streets and balconies.

I got up in the morning to go to lectures, and met Bertrand for lunch. There was the library at the Sorbonne; there were cinemas, café terraces, friends, and work. In the evening we went dancing or returned to Bertrand's room where we lay on the bed, made love, and talked for a long time in the dark. I was contented

14

enough, but there was always a part of myself, warm and alive, that longed for tears, solitude, and excitement. I thought perhaps my liver was out of order.

The Friday before going to lunch at Luc's I called to see Catherine for half an hour. She was vivacious, domineering, and always in love. I accepted rather than chose her friendship. She looked upon me as a fragile, defenceless girl, which pleased me, and I often thought her wonderful. In her eyes my indifference gave me a certain aura, as it had to Bertrand until a sudden desire to possess me got hold of him.

Just then she was infatuated with a cousin and told me a long idyllic story about him. I said I was lunching with relations of Bertrand's, and suddenly realized I had rather forgotten Luc and I regretted it. Why couldn't I recount one of those interminable love stories to amuse her? But she did not expect it. We were used to our respective roles: she talked, I listened; she gave advice and I ceased to listen.

This visit depressed me. I arrived at Luc's house without enthusiasm and in rather a panic. I would have to be polite and entertaining, and try to create a good impression, whereas I should have preferred to lunch alone, twirl a mustard-pot round in my fingers, and gaze vaguely at nothing.

Bertrand was already there, alone with Luc's wife. I saw a beautiful face which made me think of a full-blown rose. She was blonde, tall, and rather heavily built; in fact lovely, but not in a striking way. She seemed to me the type of woman whom many men would like to have to keep, one who would make them happy, a sweet woman. Was I sweet? I would ask Bertrand. I certainly held his hand and talked softly and stroked his hair. But I hated talking loudly, and I liked to smooth his hair, which felt firm and warm, like an animal's fur.

Françoise put me at ease at once. She showed me over their luxurious apartment, and settled me in an armchair with a drink. I was quite charmed with her. The embarrassment I had felt because of my old skirt and shabby sweater soon passed. Luc was expected, but was still at work. Perhaps I ought to assume some interest in his profession, which I had never thought of doing. The questions I would have liked to ask people were: 'Are you in love? What are you reading?' But I never bothered about anyone's work, though it is often of primary importance to them.

'You look worried,' Françoise said, laughingly. 'Would you like some more whisky?'

'Yes, please,' I said.

'Dominique already has the reputation of being a drunkard,' said Bertrand; 'do you know why?'

He jumped up and came over to me with an air of importance.

'Her upper lip is rather short, and when she closes her eyes to drink it gives her a look of fanaticism.'

While speaking he had taken my upper lip between his thumb and index finger. He showed me to Françoise as if I were a puppy.

I began to laugh and he let me go. Luc came in.

When I saw him I thought again how handsome he was, but this time with a sort of pang. It really hurt me to like something I could not have. I seldom wanted anything, but just then I knew that I would have liked to grasp his face in my hands, squeeze it violently between my fingers and press his full mouth against mine. Yet Luc was not really handsome. I was to hear that repeated many times afterwards, but though I had only seen him twice, there was something about his features which made his face seem a thousand times more familiar to me than Bertrand's. A thousand times less strange and a thousand times more desirable than Bertrand's, which all the same I liked.

Luc greeted us and sat down. He could be astonishingly immobile. He had something very tense in the slowness of his movements, the relaxation of his body, that made me uneasy. He looked fondly at Françoise. I looked at him. I do not remember now what we said. The conversation was mainly between Bertrand and Françoise. I cannot bear to think of those preliminaries. If at that moment I had been a little more careful to keep away from him, I could still have escaped. But now, on the contrary, I can hardly wait until I come to the first time he made me happy. Even the thought of describing my feelings fills me with a bitter, impatient joy.

We went out after lunch. In the street I immediately walked in step with Luc's rapid stride and forgot Bertrand's. Luc took my elbow to help me across the road, which embarrassed me. I did not know what to do with my forearm, nor with my hand which hung down disconsolately as though my arm had gone dead below the part he held. I did not remember how I managed with Bertrand. Later Luc and Françoise took me to a dressmaker and bought me a rust-coloured coat. In my bewilderment I hardly knew whether to refuse it or to thank them. Already there was something that seemed to race like a hurricane when Luc was there. Afterwards time suddenly dropped back to normal, and once more there were minutes, hours, and cigarettes.

Bertrand was furious with me for accepting the coat. After we left he made a violent scene.

'It's simply incredible! I suppose you'd just take anything anyone offered you!'

'It's not anyone, it's your uncle,' I said hypocritically. 'In any case, I couldn't have afforded that coat myself, it's frightfully expensive.'

'You could have done without it, I imagine?'

During the past two hours I had grown accustomed to wearing the coat, which suited me perfectly, and I was shocked by his last words. Bertrand could not understand my kind of logic and we quarrelled. In the end he took me to his room without any dinner, as if to a punishment; a 'punishment' which for him, as I well knew, was the most essential and important part of his whole day.

He trembled as he kissed me, with a respect which both touched and frightened me. How much I had preferred the carefree gaiety of our first embraces. But now, when I felt his impatience, I forgot everything and only he and I existed. It was the Bertrand I knew so well in the pleasure and agony of love. Even today, perhaps more than ever today, that pleasure seems a priceless present, and however one may mock at it, or try to reason about it, I still call it the essence of love.

3

THERE were frequent dinners, either just the four of us or with some of Luc's friends. Then Françoise went away for ten days. I loved her already. She was unfailingly kind and generous to people, and yet at moments was afraid of not understanding them, and this charmed me more than anything. She was like the earth, reassuring like the earth, and sometimes childlike. When they were together, she and Luc were very gay.

We saw her off at the Gare de Lyon. I was less shy than at first, almost natural, in fact in very good spirits. For with the complete disappearance of my boredom, to which I had not dared to give a name, I had changed for the better. I became lively and even amusing; it seemed to me that this state of things could go on for ever. I had grown used to Luc's face, and attributed the sudden emotion I sometimes felt at the sight of it to an aesthetic pleasure, or to affection.

At the door of the railway carriage Françoise smiled as she said:

'I leave him in your care.'

On the way back Bertrand stopped to buy a political journal, which would give him an excuse to get annoyed. All at once Luc turned to me and said very quickly:

'Shall we have dinner together tomorrow?'

I was about to reply: 'All right, I'll tell Bertrand,' when he cut me short: 'I'll ring you up,' and to

Bertrand who came back at that moment he said: 'Which paper have you bought?'

'I couldn't get the one I wanted,' said Bertrand. 'Dominique, we have a lecture. I think we'll have to hurry.'

He had taken my arm and continued to hold it. Bertrand and Luc eyed each other with mutual suspicion. I felt disconcerted. With Françoise gone, everything became confused and unpleasant, and Luc's first sign of interest in me remains a painful memory, for I realized I had been deliberately shutting my eyes to the truth. I badly wanted Françoise back as a protector. I realized that our quartet had existed on a false basis, for like all those who easily tell lies, I was responsive to atmosphere and sincere in playing the role I chose.

'I'll take you to the Sorbonne,' said Luc casually. He had a fast open car which he drove well. On the way we said nothing except 'See you soon' as we got out.

'As a matter of fact, I'm rather relieved Françoise has gone away,' said Bertrand; 'one can't always see the same people.'

I understood he was shutting Luc out of our future plans, but I was becoming careful, and kept quiet.

'And besides,' Bertrand went on, 'they're rather old for us, aren't they?'

I did not reply and we went in to Breme's philosophy lecture. I sat perfectly still and listened. So Luc wanted to have dinner alone with me. That was probably what happiness meant. I spread out my fingers on the wooden bench, and felt an irrepressible little smile lifting the corner of my mouth. I turned away so that Bertrand would not notice. It lasted only a moment, then I said to myself, 'you're making too much of the whole thing; it's all quite normal really. You must burn your boats, not think of the consequences, and not let yourself be taken in'; these were my natural youthful reactions.

The next day I made up my mind to treat the dinner with Luc as a frivolous adventure. I imagined his rushing in and eagerly making me a declaration. In fact, he came rather late, looking absentminded, and my one wish was that he would show some sign of agitation at our impromptu meeting. He did nothing of the sort, but talked easily about one thing and another, so that in the end I found myself following his lead. He was probably the first person with whom I had ever felt completely at ease with no mental reservations. Afterwards he suggested our going to a restaurant to dance, and took me to Sonny's. There he met friends who joined us, and I thought what a vain idiot I had been to imagine for a moment that he would have wanted to be alone with me.

When I looked round at the women at our table I realized that I was neither elegant nor witty. On the contrary, towards midnight there remained nothing of the vamp I had all day imagined myself to be, but a prostrate rag of a girl, ashamed of her dress, and longing for Bertrand, who at least thought her pretty.

Luc's friends were talking of the benefit of Alka-seltzer the morning after a party. I realized there were many people who took Alka-seltzer, and treated their bodies like precious playthings to use for their amusement and nurse with care. Perhaps I ought to abandon my books, serious conversations, long walks, and give myself over to the pleasures money can buy; to futile talk and other absorbing distractions. The thing was to possess the means to beautify myself. Did Luc care for these women, I wondered.

He turned to me, smiling, and asked me to dance. He took me in his arms, gently placed my head against his chin, and we danced. I was very conscious of his body close to mine.

'All these people bore you, don't they?' he said. 'The women do nothing but twitter.'

'I've never been to a real night-club,' I said; 'I'm dazzled.'

He began to laugh:

'How strange you are, Dominique. You amuse me. Let's go on somewhere else and talk.'

We left Sonny's. Luc took me to a bar and we began to drink deliberately. Besides liking whisky, I knew that I could only talk freely when I was a little drunk. I soon saw Luc as an agreeable and charming person, and no longer terrifying, and even felt a great tenderness for him.

Naturally we began to talk about love. He told me that it was a very good thing, less important than people made out, but that there must be a lot of love on both sides in order to be happy. I nodded. He said that he was happy because he and Françoise loved each other very much. I congratulated him, and assured him that I was not at all surprised because he and Françoise were very, very nice people. I was becoming more and more emotional.

'By the way,' said Luc, 'I would very much like to make love to you.'

I began to laugh stupidly. I felt incapable of any reaction. 'And Françoise?' I said.

'Perhaps I'll tell her. She's very fond of you, you know.'

'That's just it,' I said, 'but somehow one doesn't talk about things like that.'

I felt indignant, but my constant change from one state of mind to another was beginning to wear me out. It seemed to me both extremely natural and extremely improper that Luc wanted to sleep with me.

'In a way,' said Luc seriously, 'there is something; I mean between us. God knows I don't usually care for young girls. But we're very alike, you know. What I mean is that it wouldn't seem either silly or banal, and that is a rare thing. Well, you think it over.'

'That's it,' I said, 'I'll think it over.'

I must have been in a pitiable state. Luc leaned across and kissed my cheek.

'Poor darling,' he said, 'I'm so sorry for you. If you only had some elementary notion of morals. But you haven't, any more than I have. And you're nice, and you're fond of Françoise, and you're less bored with me than with Bertrand. That's you!'

He burst out laughing. I was annoyed. After that I always felt rather exasperated when Luc began, as he called it, to sum up the situation. Just then I couldn't help showing it.

'It doesn't matter,' he said. 'Nothing is really important in that sort of thing. I am very fond of you, I care for you, we'll have a lot of fun together, just fun.'

'I hate you!' I said.

I made my voice sound very gloomy and we both began to laugh. The complicity we had established during the past three minutes struck me as a bit dubious.

'Now I'm going to take you home,' said Luc. 'It's very late. Or if you like we'll go to the Quai de Bercy to see the sunrise.'

We went to the Quai de Bercy. Luc stopped the car. The sky was white above the Seine, which lay between the cranes like a sad child between its toys. The sky was both white and grey. It rose towards the day above the dead houses, the bridges and railway lines, slowly, indomitably, as it did every morning. Next to me Luc smoked in silence. His profile was immobile. I held out my hand, he took it, and we went slowly back towards the pension. In front of the door he let go my hand. I got out and we smiled at each other. I collapsed on to my bed, and with the thought that I ought to undress, wash my stockings, and hang up my dress, I fell asleep.

4

I AWOKE with a painful sensation of having an urgent problem to solve. For what Luc proposed was in fact a game – an alluring game – but one which would destroy a real feeling I had for Bertrand, and also something confused within myself, something complicated and bitter: for even though I might sometimes feel that all passion and all love affairs are short-lived, I was not prepared to accept this as a necessity, especially when it was imposed upon mc by Luc. Like all those who look upon life as a comedy, I could not bear to perform in one that I had not written myself.

I knew quite well that when this game was played between two people who were really attracted to each other, as a temporary solution for their loneliness, it was bound to be dangerous. It was foolish to pretend to be stronger than I was. From the moment when Luc would have 'tamed me' (as Françoise put it), and openly acknowledged me, I would be unable to leave him without suffering. Bertrand was not capable of giving me anything more than love, though I say that with affection, but where Luc was concerned, I made no such reservations. For anyhow, when one is young, nothing seems more exquisitely desirable than to take risks. I had never, so far, decided anything for myself, the choice had always been made for me. Why, this time, should I offer any resistance? There would be Luc's charm, the days to be got through, and then the evenings with him. It would all come about quite naturally; it was useless to try to see into the future.

With this blissful solution to my problems I went to the Sorbonne, where I met Bertrand and other friends and we had lunch in the Rue Cujas, and although this was a daily occurrence, that day it seemed abnormal to me. My real place was with Luc. I was puzzling it all out while Jean-Jacques, a friend of Bertrand's, made sarcastic remarks about my faraway look.

'I can't understand it, Dominique. You must be in love! Bertrand, what have you done to this absent-minded young woman, turned her into a Princesse de Clèves?'

'I don't know what you're talking about,' said Bertrand.

I looked at him. He was red in the face and avoided my glance. It was unbelievable that my friend and companion for the past year had suddenly become an adversary. I made a movement towards him. I would have liked to remind him of our summer days, our winter days, and his room, and to add that all this couldn't be wiped out in three weeks, it wasn't possible. And I would have liked him to agree vehemently with me, to reassure me, and to take me back because he loved me. But he was not a man. With certain men, amongst them Luc, one discerned a hidden strength that neither Bertrand nor any of the other very young men I knew possessed.

'Leave Dominique alone!' said Catherine in her usual dictatorial way. 'Come with me, Dominique, men are brutes; let's go and have coffee together.'

Outside she explained that I mustn't take Bertrand's attitude too seriously, for he was very attached to me, and I mustn't worry about his little fits of bad temper. I did not protest. After all, it was better for Bertrand not to be humiliated before our friends. As for me, I was sick of their speeches, their gossip, their infantile flirtations, and their tragedies, but all the same, Bertrand's suffering must be considered, and I could not ignore it. It would all happen so quickly. So far there was only a small rift between Bertrand and myself, but I knew they would begin talking about us, analysing the situation, and annoying me to such an extent that it might become a definite break.

'You don't understand,' I said to Catherine; 'it's not a question of Bertrand.'

'Ah!' she said.

I turned towards her and saw such curiosity, such a mania for interfering, and such a vampire-like expression on her face, that I began to laugh. 'I'm thinking of going into a convent,' I said gravely.

Without showing any surprise, Catherine started off on a long monologue about the pleasures of life, the little birds, the sun, etc. . . . 'all that you would be giving up for this madness.' She also spoke about more sensual pleasures, lowering her voice and whispering: 'it's just as well to talk about these things, after all, they're important!' If I had really meant what I said, she would certainly have succeeded in precipitating me into the arms of the Church by her description of the pleasures of life. Was it really possible that people only lived for 'that'? Anyhow, if I were bored, at least I was passionately bored. Besides, Catherine showed herself to be so familiar with low haunts, so anxious for promiscuous adventures, so ready with odious detailed confidences, that I was thankful to leave her standing on the pavement. Humming gaily as I walked away, I thought: 'Let's get rid of Catherine and all her attachments too!'

I wandered about for an hour, went into a lot of shops, and talked to everyone. I felt absolutely light-hearted. Paris belonged to me: Paris belonged to the unscrupulous, to the irresponsible; I had always felt it, but it had hurt because I was not carefree enough. Now it was my city, my beautiful, shining, golden city, 'the city that stands aloof'. I was carried along by something that must have been joy. I walked quickly, was full of impatience, and could feel the blood coursing through my veins. I felt ridiculously young at those moments of mad happiness and much nearer to reality and truth than when I searched my soul in my moods of sadness.

I went into a cinema in the Champs-Élysées where they showed old films. A young man came and sat down beside me. A glance showed me that he was good-looking, perhaps a little too fair. Soon he touched my elbow with his, put a hand out discreetly towards my knee: I caught it and kept it in mine. I wanted to laugh and giggle like a schoolgirl. Was this the notorious promiscuity of dark corners, the furtive, shameless embrace? I was holding the warm hand of an unknown young man in mine, although I had no use for him, and it amused me. He stroked my hand; slowly advanced one knee. I submitted with a sort of curiosity, fear, and encouragement. Like him, I was half afraid that my sense of dignity would suddenly awake, and that I would behave like an old lady who leaves her seat in disgust. My heart was beating a little fast: was it emotion or the film? The film was good, by the way. There ought to be a special place where old films are shown to people who need a friend. The young man turned a questioning face to me, and because the film

28

was very bright, I saw that he was really rather handsome. 'Yes, but not my type,' I said to myself as his face came slowly closer to mine. I thought for a moment that the people behind us must be wondering . . . he kissed well, but at the same time his hand tightened on my knee and advanced slyly, stupidly trying to gain a further advantage which so far I had not refused. I got up and went out. He must have wondered why.

I was back in the Champs-Élysées with the taste of a strange mouth on my lips, and I decided to go home and read a new novel.

It was a beautiful book by Sartre, *L'Âge de Raison*. I threw myself into it with pleasure. I was young, I liked one man and another was in love with me. I had one of those silly little girlish problems to solve. I was feeling rather important. There was even a married man involved, and another woman: a little play with four characters was taking place in the springtime in Paris. I reduced it all to a lovely dry equation, as cynical as could be. Besides, I felt remarkably sure of myself. I accepted all the unhappiness, the conflict, the pleasure to come; I mockingly accepted it all in advance.

I read on, while it gradually got dark. I put my book down, leaned my head on my arm and watched the sky turn from mauve to grey. I suddenly felt weak and helpless. My life was slipping away, and I did nothing except sneer. If only there were someone close to my cheek, whom I could keep there, whom I could press against me with love's agonized violence. I was not cynical enough to envy Bertrand, but sad enough to envy all happy lovers, all desperate meetings, all slavery. I got up and went out.

5

I WENT out several times with Luc during the two following weeks, but his friends always came too. They were, generally, travellers with entertaining stories to tell. Luc talked quickly, was amusing, and looked at me affectionately, but he always seemed distracted and pressed for time, which made me doubt whether he was really interested in me. Afterwards he drove me to my door, got out of the car, and kissed me lightly on the cheek before leaving. I was both relieved and disappointed that he no longer spoke of the desire he had said he felt for me. Finally, he announced that Françoise was returning next day, and I realized that the last two weeks had passed like a dream and I had been worrying a great deal about nothing.

We went to fetch Françoise from the station, but without Bertrand, who for the last ten days had been sulking. I was sorry for him, but took advantage of it to lead an aimless, lazy life, on my own, which suited me. I knew it made him unhappy not to see me and that prevented me being really happy myself.

Françoise arrived one morning, all smiles, kissed us, and declared that we did not look at all well, and that it couldn't have happened at a better moment, for we were invited to spend the week-end with Luc's sister, Bertrand's mother. I protested that I was not invited and had had a slight quarrel with Bertrand. Luc added that his sister exasperated him. But Françoise arranged everything. Bertrand had asked his mother to invite me, Françoise said, probably to make up this ridiculous quarrel, and as for Luc, he occasionally had to show some family feeling.

She looked laughingly at me and I smiled at her, full of goodwill. She had grown fatter, but was so warm-hearted, so trusting that I was delighted to think that nothing had happened between Luc and me and we could all three be happy together as before. We had been sensible, Luc and I. Yet as I got into the car to sit between him and Françoise I glanced at him for a second and the thought that I was renouncing him gave me a strange, disagreeable little shock. All the same I quite looked forward to seeing Bertrand again.

On a lovely evening we drove down to Bertrand's mother. I knew that when her husband died he had left her a nice country house, and the idea of going to spend a week-end somewhere satisfied a certain snobbishness in me that I hadn't had an opportunity of indulging until then. Bertrand had told me that his mother was a very charming woman. He said it in the detached way some young people assume when talking of their parents, to emphasize that their real life is elsewhere. I had gone to the expense of buying a pair of linen slacks, Catherine's being really too big for me. This purchase had exceeded my allowance, but I knew that Luc and Françoise would provide for my needs if necessary. I was astonished by my willingness to accept gifts from them, but like most people who are inclined to be indulgent towards themselves, I attributed this tendency more to their generosity than to my own weakness. It is easier to admire others than to find fault with oneself.

Luc had come with Françoise to fetch us from a café

on the Boulevard Saint-Michel. He was again looking tired and rather sad. On the open road he began to drive very fast and dangerously. Fear made Bertrand burst out laughing, and I joined in. Françoise turned round on hearing us laugh. She had the defeated look of amiable people who never dare to protest, even to protect their very lives.

'What are you laughing at?'

'They are young,' said Luc. 'Twenty is the age of hilarious laughter.'

I don't know why this phrase irritated me. I didn't like Luc to treat Bertrand and me like a couple, especially like a couple of children.

'It's nervous laughter,' I said, 'because you drive too fast and we are frightened.'

'You must come with me,' said Luc, 'and I'll teach you to drive.' It was the first time that he had used the word 'tu' to me in public. Perhaps it was only a tactless blunder. Françoise looked at Luc for a second. Then I changed my mind about it being a blunder. I didn't believe in revealing slips of the tongue, intercepted glances, and swift intuitions. There was a phrase that always surprised me in novels: 'And suddenly she knew that he lied.'

Anyhow, we were now arriving. Luc turned sharply down a little lane and I was thrown against Bertrand. He held me against him solidly, tenderly, and I felt very embarrassed. I couldn't stand Luc seeing me like that. It seemed vulgar, and rather stupid, even somewhat indelicate.

'You look like a bird,' said Françoise.

She had turned round to us. It was really a friendly look. She had not the air of an accomplice, of the mature woman who is a party to an adolescent romance. Her glance simply implied that I looked nice in Bertrand's arms and rather touching. I liked the idea of looking touching. It has often saved me from believing, thinking, or answering.

'An old bird,' I said, 'I feel quite old.'

'I do too,' said Françoise, 'but with more reason.'

Luc turned his head towards her with a little smile. I thought suddenly 'they like each other'. I expect they still make love quite often. Luc sleeps next to her, lies next to her, loves her – I wonder what he thinks about Bertrand and me. Is he in fact as jealous of him as I am of Françoise?

'Ah, here we are at the house,' said Bertrand. 'There's another car and I'm afraid my mother has some of her usual guests.'

'In that case we'll leave,' said Luc. 'I've a horror of my dear sister's friends. I know a charming little inn quite near.'

'Come along,' said Françoise, 'we've had enough grumbling. In any case, this house is charming, and Dominique doesn't know it yet. Come, Dominique.'

She took me by the hand and led me towards a rather pretty house surrounded by lawns. I thought to myself that I had just missed doing her a bad turn by deceiving her with Luc, and that I liked her very much and would hate to cause her pain, though in any case she wouldn't have known.

'Here you are at last,' said a high-pitched voice. Bertrand's mother emerged from a gap in the hedge. I had never met her. She threw me a searching glance such as mothers of young men often inflict on young girls their sons introduce to them. She seemed to be particularly blonde and flashy, and immediately started twittering round us in an exasperating way. Luc looked upon her as a calamity. Bertrand was obviously a little uncomfortable, which forced me to be specially gracious. Finally, I was relieved to find myself in my bedroom. The bed was very high with coarse sheets like the beds I had been used to in my childhood. I opened the window, which looked out on green rustling trees, and a strong smell of wet earth and grass permeated the room.

'Do you like it?' asked Bertrand.

He looked both confused and pleased and I thought that for him this week-end with me at his mother's must mean something rather important and complicated. I smiled at him.

'You've a very nice house. As for your mother, I don't know her, but she seems charming.'

'So you're pleased you came? By the way, I've got the room next to yours.'

He laughed like an accomplice and I joined in. I like strange houses and bathrooms with black and white tiles, large windows, and domineering young men. He took me in his arms and kissed me gently on the mouth. I knew his breath, his manner of kissing, and I had never told him of the young man at the cinema. He would have taken it badly. I also took it badly now. Looking back, I had a rather shameful memory of it, both comical and uneasy; altogether unpleasant. I had been in a strange mood that afternoon. I wasn't so any more.

'Come and have dinner,' I said to Bertrand, who was leaning over to kiss me again, his eyes a little dilated. I liked him to desire me. On the other hand, I didn't like myself very much.

The dinner was a deadly bore. There were, in fact, some friends of Bertrand's mother, a common-place couple. When dessert came round, the husband, who was called Richard and was chairman of some public company, made the usual remark of his generation.

'Well, young lady, are you one of these unhappy existentialists? As a matter of fact, my dear Marthe' – he was talking to Bertrand's mother – 'these disillusioned young people are beyond me. At their age, dash it, one loved life. In my time one enjoyed oneself. One went off the deep end occasionally, but at least it was amusing!'

His wife and Bertrand's mother laughed in an understanding way. Luc yawned. Bertrand prepared an answer which no one would listen to. With her natural good humour Françoise busily tried to understand why they were so boring. As for me, it was not the first time that gentlemen with pink cheeks and grey hair had aimed their healthy humour at me while masticating their food. What added piquancy to their talk was that they hadn't the faintest idea of the real meaning of the word 'existentialism'. I made no reply.

'My dear Richard,' said Luc, 'at your age, at our age I mean, I'm afraid the gay life is over. These young people make love, which is only right. One needs a girl secretary in an office to be gay.'

The gay dog did not answer. The rest of dinner passed quietly; everybody talked except Luc and myself. He was the only one who was as bored as I was, and I wondered if the incapacity to stand up to boredom was not one of the chief things we had in common.

After dinner we went on to the terrace as the weather was mild. Bertrand left us to find some whisky. Luc came over to me and told me in a low voice not to drink too much.

'At any rate, I'm behaving myself,' I said, vexed.

'I would be jealous,' he said, 'I would only want you to drink too much and say stupid things with me.'

'And the rest of the time what would I do?'

'Pull a long face as at dinner.'

'And you,' I said, 'do you think your face was gay? You don't seem to believe in the "good old times" in spite of the way you were talking.'

He laughed. 'Come and have a walk with me in the garden?'

'In the dark? What about Bertrand and the others?' I was in a panic.

'Oh, they've bored us enough. Come on, let's go.'

He took me by the arm, turning his back on the others. Bertrand hadn't yet arrived with the whisky. I thought vaguely that on his return he would rush out and try to find us under a tree and probably kill Luc as in *Pelléas et Mélisande*.

'I am taking this young girl for a stroll,' he called to them.

I didn't turn round, but heard Françoise laugh. Luc led me down a gravel path which seemed white to start with but drifted into darkness. I was suddenly very frightened. I felt I wanted to be with my parents by the River Yonne.

'I am frightened,' I said to Luc.

He didn't laugh, but took hold of my hand. I would have wished him to be always like this, silent, a little grave, protective, and tender, to say he loved me, and to take me in his arms. He stopped, and took me in his arms. I was against his suit with my eyes closed.

All the previous period had been a long escape until this very moment; his hands lifting my face, and his mouth, sweet and just made for mine. He kept his fingers round my face and held me tightly with them while we kissed. I put my arms round his neck. I was young and frightened of myself, of him, and of everything that was not the present moment. I immediately adored his mouth.

Luc didn't say a word, but kissed me, lifting his head now and then to regain his breath. I saw his face above mine in the semi-darkness like a mask, distracted and concentrated at the same time. I shut my eyes under the heat which enveloped my eyelids, my temples and throat. Something happened to me that I didn't understand, which had neither the haste nor impatience of desire, but something that was happy, slow, and thrilling.

Luc detached himself from me and I stumbled a little. He took me by the arm and we went round the garden without saying a word. I said to myself that I would like to go on kissing him until daybreak without another gesture. Bertrand so quickly exhausted his kissing. Desire rendered it useless in his eyes. It was only a step towards pleasure, instead of something lasting and sufficient in itself, as Luc made me feel it.

*

'Your garden is lovely,' said Luc, smiling at his sister.

'Unfortunately it is rather late.'

'It is never too late,' said Bertrand testily.

He looked at me. I turned my eyes away. What I wanted was to be alone in the darkness, to be able to recall and understand those few moments in the park. I would put my thoughts aside while the conversation was going on. Then later I would be up in my room with this memory. I would lie flat on my bed with my eyes wide open, would picture it all before me, and either destroy it or let it become something essential. That night I locked my door, but Bertrand did not try to come in.

6

THE morning passed slowly. Awakening had been enjoyable, like an awakening in childhood. It was not
like one of those long, dreary, and solitary days – broken up by books and study; it was the other kind. By
the other kind I mean days in which I had a part to
play, in which I had to take responsibility. The thought
of this responsibility overwhelmed me at first, and I
pressed my head into my pillow, with a feeling of physical discomfort. Then I remembered the previous evening, and Luc's kisses, and something very tender
stirred my heart.

The bathroom was most luxurious. Once in the bath
I began to sing to a gay jazz tune the words 'And now,
and now, I must make a decision.' Someone knocked
on the wall. It was Luc.

'Aren't honest folk allowed to sleep?'

He had a happy voice. Had I been born six years
earlier, before Françoise, we might have lived together
and he would have laughingly prevented me singing
in the early morning. We would have slept together.
We would have been happy for a long time, whilst now
we found ourselves in a quandary. It was a real quandary, and that is why we dared not risk getting more
deeply involved, in spite of our pretence of bored indifference. I ought to escape, to go away. I got out of
my bath, but putting on a fluffy bath-towel, which
smelt of old country cupboards, I said to myself that
the sensible thing to do was to let things run their

course and not to worry. It wasn't any good trying to analyse, I just had to wait and see.

I tried on the slacks that I had bought and glanced at myself in the looking-glass. I didn't altogether care for my appearance. My hair was untidy, but my face was pointed and had a sweet expression. I wished that I had regular features and long hair and looked romantic and sensual. These trousers were ridiculous, too narrow, and I'd never dare go down in them. It was a form of despair that I knew only too well, when I disliked my appearance so much that I would feel miserable if I decided to go out.

And then Françoise knocked, came in, and put everything right.

'My dear little Dominique, how charming you look like that! You seem even younger and more attractive than usual. You put me to shame.'

She was sitting on the bed and looking at herself in the mirror.

'I eat too many cakes because I can't resist them, and I have wrinkles too!'

She did have rather deep wrinkles round her eyes. I touched them.

'I think wrinkles are wonderful,' I said lovingly. 'Imagine all the nights, all the countries, all the faces that have gone to make even those two tiny lines. They improve you, they make you look more alive. And in any case I think they're beautiful, expressive, moving. I have a horror of smooth faces.'

She burst out laughing.

'I believe you'd ruin every beauty parlour so as to console me. You're really sweet, Dominique, very sweet.'

I was ashamed.

'I'm not as sweet as all that.'

'Do I annoy you? Young people hate to be thought sweet. But you never say anything disagreeable or unjust. And you like people. So I think you're perfect.'

'I am not.'

It was a long time since I had talked about myself. It was a game I enjoyed when I was seventeen, but now I was tired of it. In fact, only if Luc were to be interested in me or cared for me would I take an interest in myself, or care for myself, but this was a stupid thought.

'I'm exaggerating,' I said aloud.

'And you're incredibly absentminded,' said Françoise.

'Because I'm not in love,' I said.

She looked at me, and I was very tempted to say to her, 'Françoise, I am falling in love with Luc, but I'm also very fond of you. Please take him away.'

'What about Bertrand, is it really over?'

I shrugged my shoulders.

'I don't see him any more. I mean I don't look at him any more.'

'You ought perhaps to tell him?'

I did not reply. Why should I say to Bertrand, 'I don't want to see you any more,' when I didn't mind seeing him and was fond of him? Françoise smiled.

'I understand, it isn't as easy as all that. Come and have lunch. In the Rue Caumartin I saw a lovely jersey which would go beautifully with your trousers. We'll go and look at it together and . . .'

We talked gaily of clothes and walked down the stairs. The subject did not interest me very much, but I liked to talk like that to suggest a wrong adjective, make a mistake so that she could correct me, and laugh.

Downstairs, Luc and Bertrand were having lunch. They were talking of bathing.

'We might go to the swimming-pool,' Bertrand was saying. He must have thought that he could face the sunshine better than Luc. But perhaps I was mistaken.

'It's an excellent idea, and on the way I might teach Dominique how to drive.'

'No foolishness. No foolishness,' said Bertrand's mother, who came into the room draped in a sumptuous dressing-gown. 'Have you all slept well? And you, my little one?'

Bertrand looked uncomfortable. He put on a dignified expression which did not suit him. I preferred him to be gay. One likes people one is hurting to be gay. It is less upsetting.

Luc got up. He obviously could not stand his sister's presence. It made me laugh. At times I have also had these physical aversions but have been obliged to hide them. There was something childish about Luc.

'I'm going to fetch my bathing things.'

There was a scramble, everyone trying to find their things. Finally, when we were all ready, Bertrand went with his mother in their friend's car, and we three were left together.

'You drive,' said Luc.

I had some vague notions of driving and it did not work out too badly. Luc sat next to me, and Françoise, unconscious of the danger, talked from her seat in the back. I had a violent nostalgia for what might have been. Long journeys with Luc beside me, the car lights illuminating the white road at night, myself leaning on Luc's shoulder. Luc solidly at the wheel, driving too fast, the dawn on the countryside, sunsets over the sea . . .

'You know, I've never seen the sea.'

It was a surprise.

'I'll take you there,' said Luc softly, and turning towards me he smiled. It was like a promise. Françoise had not heard it and said:

'Next time we go to the sea, Luc, we must take her. She'll say, "Oh! what a lot of water! I love it!"'

'I'd probably bathe first,' I said, 'and talk about it later.'

'You know it's really lovely,' said Françoise. 'The beaches are yellow, with red rocks and all that blue sea that sweeps over them . . .'

'I adore your descriptions,' said Luc, laughing, 'yellow, blue, and red – like a schoolgirl – a young schoolgirl, of course,' he added apologetically, turning towards me. 'There are old schoolgirls, very very clever indeed. Turn right, Dominique, if you can.'

I could. We arrived in front of a lawn. In the middle of the lawn was a large swimming-pool full of blue water, the sight of which made me freeze.

We soon assembled round the pool in our bathing-suits. I met Luc coming out of his cabin and looking annoyed. When I asked him why, he said with a worried smile:

'I'm afraid I'm not very handsome.'

He wasn't. He was tall and thin, a little bent and not sunburnt. He seemed unhappy, he held his towel in front of him very carefully.

'Come, on!' I said jokingly. 'You're not as ugly as all that.'

He gave me a sidelong glance and burst out laughing.

'Young woman, you are beginning to be disrespectful.'

He plunged into the water, but came out quickly with cries of distress. Françoise sat on the side of the pool. I thought her more attractive than when she was dressed. She looked like one of the statues at the Louvre.

'It's terribly cold,' said Luc. 'One must be mad to bathe in May.'

'In April don't take off a stitch – in May do as you please,' said Bertrand's mother pompously.

But as soon as she had touched the water with her toe she went off to get dressed. I looked round the pool at our gay little group. I felt it was a pleasant occasion, but as usual could not help saying to myself: 'What are you doing here?'

'Are you going to bathe?' said Bertrand.

He stood before me on one foot and I looked at him approvingly. I knew he did dumb-bell exercises each morning. We had once spent a week-end together and, thinking I was still asleep, he had performed various exercises in front of the window – exercises that had made me laugh until I nearly cried. He had a clean, healthy look about him.

'We're lucky to have dark skins,' he said, looking at the others.

'Come on, let us get into the water,' I said. I was afraid he would begin making unpleasant remarks about his mother, who exasperated him.

I jumped into the water very reluctantly, swam round the pool so as not to be beaten, and came up with my teeth chattering. Françoise rubbed me down with a towel. I was wondering why she never had any children. She was so obviously made for motherhood, with her broad hips, well-developed body and her gentleness. It was a pity.

7

I HAD arranged to meet Luc at six o'clock two days after that week-end. It seemed that now there was something irrevocable between us. It was no longer possible to be merely frivolous. I wished I were a seventeenth-century girl and could ask for reparation for a kiss.

We were to meet at the bar in the Quai Voltaire. To my surprise, when I arrived, Luc was already there. He did not look at all well and seemed tired. I sat next to him and he immediately ordered two whiskies. Then he asked me for news of Bertrand.

'He's well.'

'Is he suffering?' He did not ask in a sarcastic tone, but very quietly.

'Why should he suffer?'

'He's not a fool.'

'I don't know why you should talk about Bertrand. It's ... well ...'

'Secondary.' He said this ironically, which maddened me.

'It's not secondary, but neither is it very important. Talking of something important, let's rather discuss Françoise.'

He burst out laughing:

'It's funny, but in this kind of situation, the partner of the other always seems a more serious obstacle than one's own. It seems a dreadful thing to say, but when you know somebody, you also know the way they suffer, and it seems more bearable. I say "bearable", but I would rather say "known", and therefore less frightening.'

'I don't know Bertrand's capacity for suffering,' I said.

'You haven't had time. I've been married for ten years, and have seen Françoise suffer. It is very disagreeable.'

For a moment we both remained quite still, probably imagining Françoise suffering. In my mind's eye I saw Françoise with her face to the wall.

'It's foolish,' said Luc at last. 'But you understand, it is not so simple as I thought.'

He took up his whisky, threw back his head, and swallowed it. It was like being at the cinema. I tried to persuade myself that this was no time to be out of touch with reality, yet everything seemed unreal to me. Luc was there, he would decide, everything was going to be all right.

He leaned forward a little, holding his empty glass and swirling the ice round and round in it. He spoke without looking at me:

'I've had affairs, naturally. Françoise mostly did not know about them except on a few unfortunate occasions. But they were never serious.' He straightened himself up in a kind of rage: 'It's not very serious for you either, but what about Françoise?'

I listened without suffering. I do not know why, but I seemed to be at a lecture on philosophy which had no reference to myself.

'But this time it is different. At the beginning I wanted you, as a man of my kind can desire a little, feline, difficult, self-willed girl. As I've already told you, I

46

wanted to possess you, to spend a night with you. I never thought . . . '

Suddenly he turned towards me, took my hands, and spoke gently. I looked closely at his face and marked every detail. I listened with passionate attention to his words, and I forgot about myself and my little inner voice.

'I never thought I would come to admire you. I do very much, Dominique. I love you very much. I can't promise to love you for "ever and ever" as children say, but we are very alike, you know. I not only want to sleep with you, I want to live with you, go away with you on a holiday. We would be very happy, very loving, I would show you the sea, teach you about money, and how to feel more free. We'd be less bored, that's all.'

'I would like that too,' I said.

'Afterwards I'd go back to Françoise. What do you risk? To get attached to me? To suffer afterwards? But after all, that's better than being bored. You'd rather be happy and even unhappy than nothing at all, wouldn't you?'

'Obviously,' I replied.

'Isn't it true that you'd risk nothing?' repeated Luc, as if to convince himself.

'Why talk about suffering?' I said. 'One must not exaggerate. I'm not so tender-hearted.'

'Good,' said Luc. 'We shall see. We'll think it over. Let's talk of something else. Would you like another drink?'

We drank each other's health. Uppermost in my mind was that we should probably go away together in a car, as I had imagined and thought impossible. And

I would take care not to get too attached to him. Knowing that the boats were burned in advance, I wasn't going to be so foolish.

Afterwards we walked along the quay. Luc laughed and talked and I laughed and talked too. I said to myself that one must always laugh with him. I felt in the right mood for it. 'Laughter and love go together,' as Alain said. It was not a question of love, but of being in harmony with each other. And besides, I was rather proud that Luc thought about me, admired me, and desired me. I could regard myself as rather special, desirable. The little keeper of my conscience, who, whenever I thought about myself, showed me a pitiable reflection, was perhaps too severe, too pessimistic?

When I left Luc I went into a bar and drank another whisky with the four hundred francs put aside for my dinner. After ten minutes I felt wonderfully kind, tender, and attractive. I looked for someone who could benefit by it, so that I could explain to him all the hard, sweet, and painful things I knew about life. I felt as if I could go on talking for hours. The barman was nice, but uninterested, so I went to the café in the Rue Saint-Jacques, where I met Bertrand. He was alone with several saucers in front of him. I sat next to him and he looked very pleased to see me.

'I was just thinking of you. There's a new bebop orchestra at the Kentucky. What if we went there? It's ages since we danced together.'

'I haven't a sou,' I said regretfully.

'My mother gave me ten thousand francs the other day, so we'll have another drink and go there.'

'But it's only eight o'clock,' I said, 'and it doesn't start till ten.'

'We'll go on drinking then,' said Bertrand gaily.

I was delighted. I enjoyed dancing difficult bebop steps with Bertrand. The juke-box was playing a jazz tune that made me move my legs in rhythm with it. When Bertrand had paid for the drinks I began to realize that he had already drunk a lot. He was in high spirits. In any case he was my best friend, my brother, and I loved him.

We did a round of bars until ten o'clock and were quite drunk at the end. Very gay, but not sentimental. When we got to the Kentucky the orchestra was starting to play. There was hardly anyone there and we had the floor to ourselves. Contrary to what I had expected, we danced well, and were very relaxed. I loved that music and the stimulus it gave me and the pleasure of following the rhythm of it with my whole body. We only sat down to drink.

'Music,' I said confidentially to Bertrand, 'jazz music gives one a heightened sense of being free from care.'

He stopped suddenly:

'That's it exactly! Most interesting. Excellent definition, bravo, Dominique!'

'But it is so,' I added.

'Awful whisky at the Kentucky! Good music, however. Music spells freedom from worry.'

'Worry about what? Listen to the trumpet. It's not only free from worry but it is necessary to the band. It was necessary to hold that note to the end. You felt it? Necessary, like love, like physical love. There's a moment when there must be ... it cannot be otherwise.'

'I quite agree, most interesting. Shall we dance?'

We spent the night dancing, drinking, and exchanging platitudes. Finally there was a vortex of faces, of feet, and there was Bertrand's arm which threw me away from him and the music which threw me back towards him, and the overwhelming heat and the suppleness of our bodies.

'It's four a.m. Closing time,' said Bertrand.

'At my home too,' I remarked.

'It doesn't matter,' he said.

It was true it did not matter. We went back to his rooms and we lay on his bed, and it was quite normal that, just as in the winter, I should feel Bertrand's familiar weight and we would be happy together.

8

HE lay beside me still asleep, his hip touching mine. It must have been early in the morning. I could not get to sleep again and I began thinking that I felt as far away from him as he was from me in his dreams. My real self seemed to be beyond the suburban houses, fields, and trees of my childhood, standing motionless at the end of a long avenue. It was as if the young girl leaning over the sleeper were a pale reflection of the calm and relentless figure whose shell I had discarded to live my own life.

I stretched myself and dressed. Bertrand woke up, questioned me, yawned, and passed his hand over his cheeks and chin, grumbling about his beard. I arranged to meet him in the evening, and went back to my room to work. But in vain. It was almost midday and atrociously hot. I was lunching with Luc and Françoise, and it was too late to start work now. I went out once more to buy a packet of cigarettes, came in, smoked one, and suddenly realized that not one of my movements had been conscious the whole morning, that during all those hours I had merely been obeying a vague instinct to carry on as usual. For me there was no reality in the wonderful smile in the omnibus, nor in the palpitating life of the streets, and I did not love Bertrand. I needed somebody or something. Lighting another cigarette, I whispered to myself 'somebody or something', and it sounded rather odd and melodramatic. So now, like Catherine, I had my moments of exaggerated sentimentality. I was in love with the word love, and all the words appertaining to it: tender, cruel, sweet, confiding, excessive, and I loved nobody, except perhaps Luc, when he was there. But since the previous day I had not dared think about him. I did not like the taste of renunciation which filled my throat when I remembered him.

I was waiting for Luc and Françoise when I felt a strange nausea which made me hurry to the basin. After it was over, I raised my head and looked at myself in the glass. I had already counted the days: 'So it has happened!' I said aloud. The well-known nightmare that I had gone through so often mistakenly was beginning again. Could it be the whisky I had drunk the night before, I wondered? In that case there was nothing to worry about. I began a grim argument with myself whilst still peering into the mirror with a mixture of curiosity and contempt. I was probably caught in a trap. I would tell Françoise; somehow she would manage to rescue me!

But I did not dare to tell Françoise. Luc gave us some wine for lunch and I grew less worried and tried to reason with myself. How was I to know whether Bertrand, who was so jealous of Luc, had not planned this in order to keep me? I thought I had all the symptoms.

The next day saw the beginning of an early summer heat-wave worse than I had ever known. I walked about the streets, because my room was unbearably hot. I asked Catherine in a roundabout way about possible solutions to my problem without daring to confess anything to her. I did not want to see Luc any more, or Françoise: they were free and strong. I was like a trapped animal, ill, and constantly breaking into hysterical laughter. I had no plans, and no strength. At the end of a week I was certain I was expecting Bertrand's child, and I began to feel calmer. I would have to do something about it. But the day before the examinations I knew that I had been mistaken and it was only a nightmare. I passed the written examination laughing with relief. I had thought of nothing else for ten days and suddenly everything became wonderful again; once more life was gay and full of possibilities.

By chance Françoise came up to my room, was horrified to find it so hot, and proposed that I should go to them to prepare my oral exam. I worked on the white carpet in their apartment, the shutters half-closed, alone. Françoise came in at about five o'clock, showed me what she had bought, questioned me a little about my work, and then we would start joking. Luc would enter the room a little later and join in our laughter. After dinner they took me home. One day that week Luc returned before Françoise. He came to where I was working and knelt down beside me on the carpet amongst my books. He took me in his arms and without a word kissed me. I rediscovered his mouth as if it had been the only one I had ever known, and as if I had been thinking of nothing else for the past fortnight. Then he told me he would write to me during the holidays, and that if I liked we could meet somewhere for a week. He caressed my neck and searched for my mouth. I longed to stay there lying against his shoulder until it got dark, perhaps complaining a little that we did not love each other. The scholastic year was over.

PART TWO

9

THE house was long and grey. A field stretched down from it to the green, sluggish River Yonne, which was guarded by flights of swallows and poplars. One in particular I loved to lie under, with my feet propped up on its trunk, looking upwards at the branches swaying in the wind. The earth smelt of warm grass and this never ceased to give me pleasure, a pleasure combined with a sense of my own helplessness. I knew that countryside in sunshine and in rain, long before I knew Paris with its streets, the Seine, and men; it was unchanging.

By some miracle I had passed my exams and now had time to read. I used to walk slowly back to the house for meals. Fifteen years earlier my mother had lost a son in somewhat tragic circumstances, and her subsequent neurasthenia had gradually become part of the house itself. The sadness that permeated the walls had assumed a pious flavour. My father tiptoed about carrying shawls for my mother.

I had a curious letter from Bertrand, full of allusions to the night we had spent together after going to the Kentucky. He said he was afraid he had been lacking in respect for me. He had not seemed to me to have been any different, and as our intimate relations had always been natural and satisfying, I could not imagine what he meant. At last I realized he was trying to insinuate that there was something of a particularly erotic nature between us which ought to bind us closer together. I thought this rather contemptible, and was annoyed with him for trying to complicate what had been the happiest and perhaps the purest side of our friendship. I understood that he was catching at a straw, so to speak, in order to avoid facing the plain truth, namely, that I did not love him any more.

I had not heard from Luc during that month. There had only been a card from Françoise to which he had added his signature. I kept telling myself, with a sort of stupid pride, that I did not love him, the proof being that I had not suffered from our separation. I did not realize that if this had been true I should have been saddened instead of triumphant. I had no patience for all these fine distinctions. I thought I had myself well under control.

I liked being in my parents' home, though logically I should have been very bored. In a way I was bored, but pleasantly, and not ashamed of it as I was with the people in Paris. I was very nice and polite to everyone, and happy to be so. It was such a relief to have nothing to do but wander from one room to another, and from one field to the next, letting the days drift idly by, and gradually acquiring a pale brown tan over face and body. I read and I waited, without waiting, for the holidays to end. They were like an enormous blank in my life.

At last, after two months, Luc's letter came. He said he would be in Avignon on the 22nd September, and would wait for me, or I could write to him there. I decided at once to go, and the past months appeared in retrospect to have been a paradise of simplicity. It was just like Luc: his quiet and apparently indifferent tone, and the ridiculous, unexpected suggestion of Avignon as a meeting place. I concocted a story for my parents, and wrote to Catherine, asking her to send me a false invitation. When it came, it was with a letter expressing her surprise, as Bertrand was in the south of France with some of our friends, and who else would I be meeting? Catherine was very upset at my lack of confidence in her, and she knew of no reason which would justify it. I wrote her a few words of thanks, telling her that if she wished to hurt Bertrand, she had only to mention my letter, which she did, out of friendship to him, of course.

Carrying a small suitcase, I took the train to Avignon, which was fortunately on the line to the coast. My parents saw me off. Without knowing why, I had tears in my eyes. It seemed to me that for the first time I was leaving my childhood, with its familiar security, behind, and I already hated Avignon.

After Luc's long silence and the cool tone of his letter I had a picture of him as rather hard and indifferent and I arrived at Avignon prepared to be on my guard, not a favourable attitude for a lovers' meeting. I was not going away with Luc because he loved me, nor because I loved him, but because we understood and liked each other. On second thoughts these reasons seemed insufficient, and the whole trip terrifying.

But once again Luc surprised me. He was waiting on the station platform looking very worried, but as soon as he saw me his face lighted up. When I got off the train he put his arms round me and kissed me lightly.

'You look marvellous! I'm so glad you've come.'

'You too,' I said, referring to his appearance. He was thinner, sunburnt, and much better looking than in Paris.

'There's no reason why we should stay in Avignon. Let's go and have a look at the sea; that is what we're here for. Later we'll decide what we want to do.'

His car stood in front of the station. He threw my suitcase into the back and we drove off. I felt completely stunned and, perversely enough, a little disappointed because he was so unlike what I had expected. I hadn't remembered him so seductive nor so gay.

The road was beautiful, bordered with plane-trees. Luc smoked, and we raced along in the sunshine with the hood down. I said to myself: 'Well, here I am, it is really happening!' And it meant nothing to me, absolutely nothing. I might just as well have been sitting under my poplar tree with a book. My lack of comprehension for what was actually taking place soon struck me as funny, and I asked Luc for a cigarette. He smiled.

'Better now?'

I began to laugh.

'Yes, much better. I'm wondering what I am doing here beside you, that's all.'

'You're not doing anything: you're out for a drive, you're smoking, you're wondering if you are not going to be rather bored. Would you like me to kiss you?'

He stopped the car, took me by the shoulders, and kissed me. For us, this was a very good beginning. I smiled a little, and we continued on our way. He was holding my hand. He understood me. For two months I had been living with people who were semi-strangers, who existed in an atmosphere of perpetual mourning which I did not share, and now it seemed that life was slowly beginning again.

The sea was a great surprise to me. For a moment

I regretted that Françoise was not there so that I could tell her that it really was blue with red rocks and yellow sands and that it looked marvellous. I was a little afraid Luc might show it to me with an air of triumph, while he watched my reactions, which would have forced me to answer in superlatives, but he just pointed to it with a finger when we reached Saint-Raphael:

'There's the sea!'

We drove on slowly through the evening, the sea gradually fading to grey. At Cannes, Luc stopped the car on the Croisette in front of a gigantic hotel. The entrance-hall terrified me. I knew that before I could feel at ease I would have to get accustomed to all this grandeur, all the lackeys, and transform them into familiar sights, which would no longer be a menace to me. I wished I were far away. Luc, who was conferring with a haughty-looking man behind a desk, noticed my discomfort, and guided me through the hall with a hand on my shoulder. The room was immense, almost white, with two balcony doors overlooking the sea. There was a confusion of porters, luggage, windows and cupboards being opened. I stood in the middle of it with dangling arms, disgusted at my incapacity to react.

'Here we are,' said Luc.

He gave a satisfied glance at the room and went out on to the balcony.

'Come and have a look.'

I leaned on the balustrade beside him, but kept a respectable distance. I had no desire to look out, nor to be so familiar with this man I hardly knew. He glanced briefly at me: 'Now look here, you little savage, go and have a bath and then come and have a drink with me. In your case I think the only remedies are comfort and alcohol.'

He was right. I came back when I was dressed, with a glass in my hand, complimented him on all his arrangements, on the bathroom and the sea. He told me I was looking very pretty. I answered that he was very good-looking, and we surveyed the crowd and the palms with satisfaction. Then he went in to change, leaving me with a second whisky, and I walked about barefoot on the thick carpet humming to myself.

Dinner was very pleasant. We talked sensibly and affectionately of Françoise and Bertrand. I hoped I wouldn't meet Bertrand, but Luc said we were sure to run into someone who would be delighted to be able to tell him and Françoise that they had seen us, and that we should put off worrying about it until we were back in Paris. I was touched that he took such a risk for my sake. I yawned because I was dead tired, and I added that I admired the way he took everything in his stride.

'It's wonderful! You make up your mind to do a thing, you do it, and accept the consequences, you're not afraid.'

'What should I be afraid of?' he asked with a strange sadness in his voice. 'Bertrand won't kill me, Françoise won't leave me, you won't love me.'

'Perhaps Bertrand will kill me, though,' I said crossly.

'He's much too kind,' said Luc. 'In fact, everyone is kind.'

'It's the bad ones who cause the most trouble, isn't that what you once said?'

'Quite right. But it's late, come to bed.'

He said it quite naturally. Our conversation had been

far from passionate, and that 'come to bed' seemed to me rather bold. To tell the truth I was frightened, very frightened of the night before me.

In the bathroom I put on my pyjamas with trembling hands. They were like schoolgirl's, but I had no others. When I entered the room Luc was already in bed. He was facing the window, smoking. I slipped in beside him. He stretched out his hand and took mine. I was shivering.

'Take off your pyjamas, little idiot, you'll get them all crushed. How can you be cold on a night like this? Are you ill?'

He took me in his arms, carefully peeled off my pyjamas, and threw them in a heap on the floor. I remarked that they would get crushed all the same. He laughed gently. All his movements had become very gentle. He gently kissed my shoulders and my mouth, while he continued to talk:

'You smell of warm grass. Do you like this room? Otherwise we'll go somewhere else. Cannes is a nice place. . . .'

I answered 'Yes, yes' in a strangled voice. I was longing for it to be tomorrow morning. It was not until he moved a little away from me and placed a hand on my side that I became really concerned. He caressed me and I kissed his neck, his chest, everything I could touch of that black shadow outlined against the window. I put my hands on his back; we sighed. Then I saw nothing more. I was dying, I was about to die, and yet I did not die, but I swooned. The rest of the world faded into insignificance, as it always will.

When we separated, Luc opened his eyes and smiled at me. I fell asleep immediately, with my head on his arm.

10

I HAD always heard that it is very difficult to live with anyone and I believed it in theory, though I did not actually experience it during the short time I spent with Luc. I thought it must be true, because I never felt at my ease with him: I was afraid of his being bored. Usually I am more frightened of being bored myself than of boring others, but in this case the situation was reversed, and I found it rather a strain. How could Luc be difficult to live with, considering that he said very little and did not even ask me what I was thinking about, as most people do? He invariably looked pleased to have me with him, made no demands on me, and showed no signs either of indifference or passion. We walked in step, had the same tastes, the same rhythm of life; we liked being together, and all went well between us. I did not even regret too much that he could not make the tremendous effort needed to love someone, to know them, and to dispel their loneliness. We were friends and lovers. We bathed in the too-blue Mediterranean together, lunched almost in silence, stupefied by the sun, and then returned to the hotel. Sometimes as I lay in his arms in that moment of great tenderness that follows love-making I longed to say: 'Luc, love me, let's try, do try!' but I never did. I confined myself to kissing his eyes, his mouth, all the features in that new face which the lips discover after the eyes have feasted on it. I had never loved a face so much. I even loved his cheeks: that part of the face which, until then, had always seemed lifeless to me, fish-like. When I laid my face against Luc's cool cheek, a little roughened by the growing bristles, I understood why Proust had written at such length of Albertine's cheeks. He also taught me to know my body, and talked quite dispassionately about it, as of something precious. Sensuality was not the basis of our relationship, but something else, a strange bond that united us against the weariness of playing a part, the weariness of talking, in short: weariness itself.

After dinner we always strolled round to the same rather sinister little bar behind the Rue d'Antibes. There was a small band, and when we first went there Luc asked them to play 'Lone and Sweet' for me, as he knew I liked it. Afterwards he turned to me with an air of triumph:

'Is that the tune you wanted?'

'Yes, it's nice of you to have thought of it.'

'Does it remind you of Bertrand?'

I answered that it did, a little, but that the record had been in every juke-box for ages. He looked rather cross.

'What a pity, we'll have to find another.'

'Why?'

'When one has a love affair there must be a special tune, a perfume, something to remind one of it for the future.'

My expression must have amused him, for he began to laugh:

'At your age one never thinks of the future. I'm looking forward to a pleasant old age, with my records.'

'Have you many?'

'No.'

'What a pity!' I exclaimed. 'If I were your age I should probably have a whole library of them.'

He took my hand.

'Are you offended?'

'No, but all the same, it seems strange to think that in a few years' time, a whole week of my life, that I lived with a man, will have been reduced to a gramophone record; especially when that man is quite certain of it and says so.'

I was so irritated that tears came into my eyes. It was the way he had said 'are you offended?' When people used a certain tone towards me it always made me feel like crying.

'Otherwise I'm not offended,' I said in a shaky voice.

'Let's dance,' said Luc.

He took my arm and we began to dance to Bertrand's tune, which was not nearly so well played as on the records.

While we were dancing, Luc suddenly held me very close, I suppose to show his violent affection. I, too, clung to him. Then he let me go and we spoke of other things. We soon found a tune that suited us, which was quite easy because it was being played everywhere. Except for that slight argument I behaved very well; I was gay, and thought our little adventure was proving a great success. Besides, I admired Luc. I could not help admiring his intelligence, his equilibrium, his virile way of giving to each thing its right weight and importance, without being either cynical or complacent. Sometimes in exasperation I wanted to say to him: 'Why can't you love me? It would be so much more restful for me.' But I knew this was impossible. Ours was more an affinity than a passion, and neither of us could ever bear to be dominated by the other. Luc had neither the opportunity, the strength, nor the desire for a closer relationship.

The week we had planned was nearly over, but Luc said nothing about leaving. We had become very brown, but were tired after nights spent in the bar, talking, drinking, and waiting for the dawn: the pale dawn over an inhuman sea, the motionless boats, the mad, graceful crowd of gulls roosting on the hotel roof. We went back at dawn, greeted the same sleepy porter, and Luc took me in his arms and loved me in a state of semi-intoxication and fatigue. We woke at midday for our bathe.

That morning, which would have been our last, I imagined he was in love with me. He walked about the room with a thoughtful expression that intrigued me.

'What did you tell your family? When did you say you were coming back?'

'I told them in about a week.'

'If you like, we could stay on another week.'

'Yes,' I said. 'Do let's.'

I realized I had not seriously thought about leaving. I would pass my life in that hotel which had become so hospitable, so comfortable, like a great ship. All my nights with Luc would be sleepless, we would drift slowly from summer to winter, and towards death, always talking of the temporary nature of our stay.

'But I thought Françoise was expecting you?'

'I can arrange that,' he said. 'I don't want to leave Cannes, or you.'

'Neither do I,' I said quietly.

For a moment I imagined that perhaps he loved me,

67

but did not want to tell me so. It made my heart miss a beat. Then I thought, what did words matter, he cared for me, and that was enough. We were going to have one more happy week together. Afterwards I would have to leave him. But why, for whom, for what? To go back to my usual boredom and loneliness? Now, when he looked at me, it was his face I saw; when he spoke, it was he I tried to understand. He it was who interested me, whose happiness I had at heart: Luc, my lover.

'It's a good idea,' I said. 'To tell you the truth, I hadn't thought about leaving.'

'You never think of anything,' he said with a laugh.

'Not when I'm with you,' I said.

'Why? Do you feel so young and irresponsible?'

He smiled mockingly. If I had shown him that I wanted it otherwise he would soon have changed his 'little girl and her protector' attitude. Fortunately I felt quite adult, even rather blasé.

'No,' I said, 'I feel perfectly responsible. But what am I supposed to be responsible for? There is only myself, and my own life, which, after all, is simple enough. Still, I am not unhappy, I'm sometimes even contented, but never really happy. I am nothing, except when I'm with you, and then I'm all right!'

'That's good!' he said, 'I feel the same with you.'

'Let's start purring!'

He began to laugh:

'You're like a cat with its back up as soon as you think you might be deprived of your absurd little dose of daily despair. I should hate to make you "purr", as you say. I don't want you to be "in heaven" when you are with me, it would bore me to extinction.'

'Why?'

'I'd feel lonely. That is the only time I'm ever frightened by Françoise: when she's next to me, saying nothing, and feeling satisfied. On the other hand, it is very satisfying to a man to feel he has made a woman happy, even if he can't imagine why.'

'Well, what could be better?' I said quickly. 'When we get back, you'll make Françoise happy, and me a little unhappy.'

I regretted my words as soon as I had spoken. He turned to me:

'You, unhappy?'

'No,' I said, smiling, 'only somewhat bewildered. I shall have to find somebody to look after me, and no one could do it as well as you.'

'I'd rather not know about it,' he said angrily. Then he thought again: 'Yes, you had better tell me. You must always tell me everything. If the fellow is troublesome, I'll thrash him, otherwise I'll sing his praises, like a real father.'

He took my hand, turned it over, and kissed the palm very gently. I put my free arm round his neck. I thought how young he still was, how vulnerable, and how kind: this man with whom I was having an unsentimental love affair with no future. And he was honest.

'We're both honest people,' I said sententiously.

'Yes,' he said, laughing, 'but don't smoke your cigarette like that if you want to look like an honest woman!'

I drew myself up in my spotted dressing-gown:

'Well, if I'm an honest woman, what am I doing here, dressed in this way in a palace hotel with another woman's husband? Am I not a typical example of one of those vicious young ladies from Saint-Germain-des-Prés who break up marriages as a hobby?'

'Yes, and I'm the model husband, who has been led astray by my senses. I am the victim, the unhappy victim! Come to bed.'

'No,' I said, 'I refuse. I have lighted the flame, but I will not be the one to extinguish it, so there!'

He collapsed on to the bed with his head in his hands. I sat next to him, looking grave, and when he raised his head I fixed my eyes on him severely.

'I'm a vamp!'

'And what am I?'

'A miserable human wreck, who was once a man. . . . Luc, we have another week!'

I threw myself down beside him. I entwined my hair with his. His skin was warm and fresh against mine, he smelt of the sea and salt.

*

I was lying on a deck-chair near some elderly English ladies facing the sea in front of the hotel. It was eleven o'clock in the morning. Luc had to go to Nice on business, and although I liked Nice, at least the old part, between the station and the Promenade des Anglais, I had refused to go with him because I suddenly longed to be by myself.

So there I was, yawning (for I was exhausted from lack of sleep) and extremely comfortable. My hand trembled a little as I struck a match to light my cigarette. The September sun, no longer very hot, caressed my cheek. For once I was delighted to be alone. 'We're only happy when we're tired,' Luc once said, and it was true that I was one of those people who are only happy once they have subdued that part of their vitality which continually makes demands and always feels misgivings: the part which asks 'What have you done with your life? What are you going to make of it?' Questions to which I could only reply 'Nothing.'

A very beautiful young man passed by at that moment. My glance travelled over him with a new and wonderful indifference. Usually I was rather embarrassed by beauty that seemed to me too blatant and inaccessible. The young man, though his appearance was so pleasing, did not exist for me. Luc was the only man who was real for me, but I was not the only woman for him. He looked at them complacently, but without comment.

Suddenly I could only see the sea through a mist. I was suffocating. I felt my forehead, it was soaked with perspiration and the roots of my hair were damp. A drop ran slowly down my spine. Perhaps death was like this: a blue mist into which one gradually sinks. I would not have offered any resistance to death at that moment.

The thought had come into my mind for a fleeting second. I seized upon it: 'I would not mind dying.' All the same, there were things I cared for: Paris, the scent of flowers, books, love, and the life I was living with Luc. I had the feeling I would never again be so happy as with him. He had been meant for me since the beginning of time, and if there were such a thing as destiny, then we had been fated to meet. My destiny was that Luc would leave me, and I would have to try to start all over again with someone else, but I would never again feel as I did with him: so tranquil, so little alone, and so free to say what I thought, knowing he would understand. But he was going back to his wife, leaving me to my room in Paris, to those interminable afternoons, my moments of despair, and to my unsatisfactory love affairs. I began to weep out of self-pity.

After a few minutes I blew my nose. Sitting quite near me I noticed an elderly Englishwoman staring fixedly at me. I felt myself blushing. Then I looked more carefully at her. I was filled with respect: here was another human being, she was looking at me and I at her, both staring hard at each other in the sunshine, both almost on the threshold of some great revelation, two human beings, not even speaking the same language, two perfect strangers. Soon she got up and, leaning heavily on a stick, limped away.

Happiness is like a flat plain without landmarks. That is why I have no precise memories of my stay in Cannes except those few unhappy moments, Luc's laughter, and the pathetic scent of fading mimosa in our room at night. Perhaps, for people like myself, happiness signifies a bolder attitude towards the tedium of everyday existence. Just then I realized so well what it meant to me. For when I met Luc's glance I felt that all was well with my world, he was taking my worries off my shoulders. When he smiled at me, I knew why he was smiling, and felt like smiling too.

I remember an exciting moment one morning. Luc was lying on the sand, while I was diving from a raft. I climbed up to the highest board. I could see Luc and the crowds on the beach, and below me the calm water, into which I was about to fall as though it were silk. I would be falling from a great height, and during my descent I would be alone, terribly alone. Luc was watching me. He made an ironical gesture to pretend he was frightened, and I let myself go. The sea rose up to meet me and I hurt myself as I dived in. I swam ashore and collapsed on the sand next to Luc, sprinkling him with water. I laid my head on his dry back and kissed his shoulder.

'Are you crazy, or just trying to set up a record?' he asked.

'Crazy,' I answered.

'That was my proud thought when I saw you diving from so high in order to come back to me. It made me very happy.'

'Are you happy? I am. I must be because I never have to ask myself the question. That's an axiom, isn't it?' All I could see of him was his firm brown neck because he was lying face downwards. 'Anyway, I'm returning you to Françoise in good condition.'

'Cynic!' he answered.

'You are far less cynical than we are,' I replied. 'Women are very cynical. You're just a little boy compared with Françoise and me.'

'Don't be so pretentious.'

'You men are more pretentious than we are,' I said. 'Pretentious women are merely ridiculous; in men it takes the form of a sham virility which they exploit in order to . . .'

'Have you finished with all your axioms? Talk to me about the weather, it's the only subject permitted on holidays.'

'It is very, very fine,' I said, and turning on to my back, I went to sleep.

When I woke up, the sky was overcast, the beach deserted, and I was utterly exhausted. Luc was sitting beside me fully dressed, smoking and looking at the sea. I watched him for a moment without revealing that I was awake. For the first time I felt a purely objective curiosity about him: 'what can he be thinking of?' I wondered, 'what does a human being think about on an empty beach, facing an empty sea, beside someone fast asleep?' I put out my hand and touched his arm. He did not even start. He was never startled, rarely surprised, and seldom raised his voice.

'So you've woken up?' he said lazily. He stretched himself. 'It's four o'clock.' I sat up.

'Four o'clock? Do you mean to say I've been asleep for four hours?'

'Don't get excited,' said Luc. 'We have nothing particular to do.'

His words struck me as ominous. It was true we had nothing to do when we were together, no work, no friends in common. 'Do you regret it?' I asked him.

He turned to me and smiled. 'I love it! Put on your sweater, darling, you'll catch cold. Let's have tea at the hotel.'

The Croisette was gloomy now the sun had gone in; a slight breeze stirred the ancient palms, the hotel seemed to be asleep. We had tea brought up. I had a hot bath and then lay down beside Luc, who was reading on the bed, from time to time flicking the ash from his cigarette. We had closed the shutters to exclude the grey sky outside: the room was warm and cosy. I lay on my back with my hands crossed on my stomach like a corpse or a fat man. I shut my eyes. The only sounds were the rustle of pages as Luc turned them and the distant splash of waves.

I was thinking: 'I am close to Luc, lying beside him.

74

I have only to put out my hand to touch him. I am familiar with his body, his voice, the way he sleeps. Now he's reading and I'm just a little bored, but it's not disagreeable. Soon we'll be having dinner, then we shall go to bed, and in three days we must part. It will probably never again be like this. But this moment is ours. I don't know if it is love, or whether we just harmonize, and it is not important. We are alone, but separate. He has no idea I am thinking of us; he's reading. But we're together, and I have all he can give me either of his warmth or indifference. In six months, when we shall perhaps no longer meet, I shall have forgotten this moment and only remember others, involuntary, vague and silly ones perhaps, and yet this is the moment I shall probably have loved most, the one when I accepted that life was just what it seemed, both peaceful and heart-rending.' I stretched out my arm and took the book away from Luc. It was *La Famille Fenouillard*, and he was always telling me I ought to read it. I began to laugh, and he joined in while we read together, cheek to cheek, and soon mouth to mouth, the book at last falling to the floor, pleasure enveloping us like the night over Cannes.

*

At last came the day of departure. We had avoided all mention of it during the last evening because we were both afraid, he that I would become sentimental, and I, that, feeling he was half-expecting it, I would give way. During the night I woke up several times in a panic and felt for him, to make sure he was still there, sleeping beside me. And on each occasion, as if he had been on the watch, or as if he were sleeping so lightly that he was conscious of my fears, he took me in his arms, put a hand on my neck, and murmured: 'There, there,' as one does to reassure an animal. It was a warm night of half-sleep, broken by whispers, heavy with the scent of the mimosa we were leaving behind us. Then came the morning and breakfast, and Luc packed his bag. I did mine at the same time, and we discussed the route we would take and the restaurants on the way. I was annoyed with myself for pretending to be calm and brave when I was not brave, and saw no reason why I should be. I felt nothing except perhaps a vague unease. For once we were each playing a part. I thought it wiser to stick to it, for I did not want to start suffering before I left him; far better to adopt the attitude, the movements, and the face of decent mediocrity.

'Well, are we ready?' he said at last. 'I'll ring for them to fetch the luggage.'

I became fully conscious of the moment.

'Let's go out on to the balcony for the last time,' I said in a melodramatic voice.

He looked upset, then, seeing my expression, began to laugh.

'You're a tough nut, a cynic. I like you.'

We were standing in the middle of the room. He put his arms round me and shook me gently: 'You know it is a rare thing to be able to say to someone: 'I like you,' after two weeks' cohabitation.'

'It wasn't cohabitation,' I protested laughing; 'it was a honeymoon.'

'All the more reason,' he said, moving away from me.

At that moment I felt he was leaving me, and I

76

longed to hold him back by the lapels of his coat. It was a fleeting thought, and it shook me.

On the return journey I drove part of the way. Luc said we would arrive in Paris during the night, that he would ring me up the next day, and he would arrange a lunch with Françoise, now home after two weeks in the country with her mother. I didn't like the idea of meeting Françoise so soon, but Luc told me to say nothing about our trip and that he would arrange everything with her. I could see myself spending the autumn with them both, and meeting Luc sometimes for a stolen kiss or a night. I had never counted on his leaving Françoise, first because he had warned me, and then because I realized it was out of the question to hurt her. Even if he had offered to do so, I would probably not have accepted it at that moment.

He told me he had a lot of work waiting to be dealt with, but that he was not very interested in it. As for me, the new term was beginning, and I would have to go on with the studies that had so depressed me before. We were both in low spirits when we reached Paris, but I did not mind because it was the same for both of us: the same discouragement, the same weariness, and consequently the same necessity to hold on to each other.

We arrived in Paris late in the night. At the Porte d'Italie I glanced at Luc, who looked tired, and I thought that we had managed our little escapade very well. After all, we were adult, civilized, and reasonable. I suddenly felt furiously, horribly humiliated.

PART THREE

II

Paris was never strange to me when I returned to it, I always felt at home there. Once again I was captivated by its charm as I walked about the streets, still deserted after the summer. Paris distracted me during the three long empty days of Luc's absence. I was always searching for him, and seeking his hand at night, and each time not finding him seemed unnatural and unnecessary. In retrospect the two weeks with him appeared to me both satisfying and bitter. Strangely enough, I had no sense of defeat, but rather one of achievement, and this, I realized, would make it difficult, and perhaps painful for me to hope for any similar experience.

Bertrand would soon be home. What should I say to him? I knew he would try to get me back. Should I renew our intimacy? And, above all, how could I bear the close contact of anyone but Luc?

Luc did not telephone the following day, nor the day after. I attributed this to complications with Françoise and felt rather important, but also ashamed. I walked a great deal, and thought in a vague way about the coming year. Perhaps I could find something more interesting to work at than law? Luc had said he wanted to introduce me to one of his friends, the editor of a newspaper. Until then, with my usual inertia, I had resorted to sentimentality as a compensation for my troubles; now I looked to a profession instead.

After two days I could no longer resist the desire to see Luc. Not daring to telephone, I sent a little note, asking him to ring me up. He did so the following day, and said he had fetched Françoise from the country and could not telephone to me before. His voice sounded rather strained. I thought it was because he missed me. When, a moment afterwards, he told me so, I had a vision of a café where we would meet, and he would take me in his arms, saying he couldn't live without me, that the past two days had been unbearable. I would have replied truthfully that I felt the same and left the decision to him. But when we actually met in a café, he told me that Françoise was well, that she had asked no questions, and that he was overwhelmed with work. He said: 'You look lovely!' and kissed the palm of my hand.

I found him changed by his dark suit, and attractive. His face looked sharpened and tired. It seemed strange that he was no longer mine. I was already beginning to think that I had not really 'benefited' (I disliked the word) by my stay with him. I talked quite cheerfully, and so did he, but we were both unnatural: perhaps because we were surprised that one can so easily live together for two weeks without anything serious happening. When he got up I felt suddenly indignant, and almost said to him: 'Where are you going? Are you leaving me alone?' He left, and I was alone. I had nothing much to do. I thought: 'How silly all this is!' and shrugged my shoulders. I walked about the streets for an hour, went into one or two cafés, hoping to meet some friends, but no one had come back yet. I could still go and spend a fortnight on the Yonne, but as I was to dine with Luc and Françoise two days later, I decided only to go away after that.

I spent those two days at the cinema or on my bed,

sleeping and reading. My room seemed unfamiliar to me. The night of the dinner I dressed carefully and went to their house. As I rang the bell I had a moment of fear, but Françoise came to open the door herself and her smile reassured me at once. I knew, just as Luc had told me, that she would never be ridiculous, and never play a role that was not in keeping with her great kindness and dignity. She had never been betrayed, and never would be.

It was a curious meal. There we were, the three of us, and everything was as before, only we had drunk a good deal. Françoise appeared to know nothing, but I thought she looked at me more attentively than usual. From time to time, Luc spoke to me, looking into my eyes, and I made a point of answering gaily and naturally. The conversation turned upon Bertrand, who was expected back the following week. 'I shan't be here,' I said.

'Where will you be?' said Luc.

'I'm probably going to stay a few days with my parents.'

'When will you be back?' (It was Françoise who asked me.)

'In a fortnight.'

'Dominique, I simply must call you "tu",' she said. 'It's ridiculous to go on saying "vous" to you.'

'Let's all call each other "tu",' said Luc, with a laugh, and he went over to the gramophone. My eyes followed him, and as I turned back to Françoise I saw that she was watching me. I stared back, feeling rather uneasy, but determined not to appear to be avoiding her glance. She put her hand over mine for a moment with a sad little smile which upset me:

'You'll send us a postcard, won't you, Dominique? You haven't told us yet how your mother is?'

'Very well,' I said. 'She . . .'

I stopped because Luc had put on the tune that was played everywhere in Cannes, and suddenly it all came back to me with a shock. He had not turned round. For a moment I felt in a panic between Françoise's complacence, which was not genuine, and Luc's unreal sentimentality. It was all such a muddle. I longed to run away.

'I like that tune,' said Luc quietly.

He sat down, and I realized that he had been thinking of nothing, not even of our bitter little dispute about keeping records as souvenirs. It was just that the tune must have been going round in his head, and he had bought the record to get it out of his system.

'I like it very much too,' I said.

He raised his eyes to me, remembered, and smiled so tenderly and openly that I lowered mine. Françoise lit a cigarette. I was quite bewildered. Our situation could not even be regarded as false, for surely we need only have mentioned it, for each one to have offered advice, calmly and objectively, as if the matter did not concern ourselves.

'Well, are we going to that play or not?' asked Luc, and he turned to explain to me, 'We've been invited to see a new play. We could all go.'

'Oh, yes,' I said. 'Why not?' I nearly added, with a burst of hysterical laughter: 'the more the merrier.'

Françoise took me to her room to try on one of her coats, more elegant than mine. She put on one or two, and turned me about to see the effect with the collar up. At one moment she was holding it against my face

84

with both hands, and in my hysterical state I thought: 'I'm at her mercy; perhaps she's going to strangle me or bite me.' But she only smiled:

'You're rather lost in it.'

'Quite true,' I answered, not thinking of the coat.

'I simply must see you when you come back.'

That's it, I thought. She's going to ask me not to see Luc any more. Could I agree? I knew that the answer was I could never give him up.

'I've decided to look after you,' Françoise went on, 'to help you to dress better, and to show you something more amusing than all those students and college libraries.'

Oh, good heavens! I thought. This is really not the right moment to say such a thing.

'Wouldn't you like it?' she said, when I did not reply. 'I always feel you might be my daughter' – she said it half-laughing, but kindly – 'even if you are a bundle of nerves and only interested in the intellectual side of life . . .'

'It's too sweet of you,' I said, emphasizing the 'too'. 'I don't know what to do.'

'Leave it all to me,' she said, smiling.

I've got myself into a nice mess, I thought, but if Françoise likes me, and wants to see me, I'll be able to be with Luc oftener. Perhaps I could tell her about him. Perhaps she wouldn't mind much after ten years of marriage.

'What makes you like me so much?' I asked.

'You have the same kind of nature as Luc. You both have a tendency to be unhappy, and need the consolation of a Venus like me. There's no escape for you!'

In imagination I gave up the struggle. Luc was in a very good mood at the theatre. Françoise pointed everyone out to me, and told me all the scandal about each. They took me back to my pension, and Luc openly kissed the palm of my hand, leaving me rather flustered. I soon fell asleep, and the next day I took the train to the Yonne.

12

But the Yonne was grey, and I was intolerably bored. It was not only boredom now, but a longing for someone. At the end of a week I went back to Paris. As I was leaving, my mother suddenly woke up and asked me if I were happy. I assured her that I was, that I liked studying law, was working hard, and had many friends. Reassured, she left me, and returned once more to her melancholy. Not for a moment had I felt the least desire to confide in her as I had the year before. Besides, what could I have told her? I was definitely growing up.

At the pension I found a note from Bertrand asking me to telephone as soon as I returned. No doubt he wanted an explanation from me (I had not much faith in Catherine's discretion) and I owed him that at least. I rang him up and we arranged to meet. In the meantime I went to register at the university restaurant.

At six o'clock I met Bertrand at the café in the Rue Saint-Jacques, and it seemed as though nothing had happened, and everything would begin again. But as soon as he got up and deferentially kissed my cheek I was recalled to reality. I tried in a feeble way to appear light-hearted and frivolous.

'You've grown better-looking,' I said with real sincerity, and with the cynical little thought: what a pity!

'You too,' he said shortly. 'I wanted you to know: Catherine told me everything.'

'What about?'

'Your stay on the Riviera. I imagine you were with Luc, weren't you?'

'Yes,' I said. I was surprised to notice that he did not appear angry, but calm, and rather sad.

'Well, there you are. I'm not a person to be satisfied with a half-share. I still love you: enough to be able to forgive you, but not enough to allow myself the luxury of being jealous, and of being made to suffer again as I did this spring. You must choose between us.'

He had said it all in one breath.

There was no question of a choice. I was in a quandary. According to Luc I had never considered Bertrand as a problem.

'Either you give up seeing Luc, and we go on as we were, or you see him, and we'll just remain good friends, that's all.'

'I see.' I could not think of anything to say. He seemed to have become more mature and serious. I almost admired him. But he meant nothing to me, absolutely nothing. I laid my hand on his:

'I'm really very sorry,' I said, 'I cannot give him up.'

He remained silent for a moment, looking out of the window.

'It's hard for me,' he said.

'I hate to hurt you,' I went on. I was really distressed.

'That's not the worst part,' he said, as if talking to himself. 'When one has made a decision it's all right. It's when one still hangs on . . .' He turned to me. 'Do you love him?'

'Of course not,' I said, irritated. 'There's no ques -tion of that. We get on very well, that's all.'

'If you are ever in trouble, I'm here,' he said. 'And

I think you will be. You'll see. There's nothing to Luc. He's just a depressive intellectual, no more.'

I thought of Luc's tenderness and his laughter with a surge of joy.

'Believe me.' He added with a sort of excitement: 'In any case I'll always be available, you know, Dominique. I've been very happy with you.'

We were both on the point of tears. He, because everything was over and he must still have had some hope, and I because I felt I was losing my natural protector in order to embark on an unknown adventure. I got up and kissed him lightly:

'Goodbye, Bertrand. Forgive me.'

'Yes, please go!' he said gently.

I left feeling completely demoralized. What a prospect for the New Year!

Catherine was waiting in my room sitting on the bed with a tragic air. She got up when she saw me and held out her hand. I took it without enthusiasm, and sat down.

'I came to apologize, Dominique. Perhaps I ought not to have said anything to Bertrand? What do you think?'

I admired her for asking the question.

'It doesn't matter. It might have been better for me to have told him myself, but it's of no importance.'

'Good.' She sighed with relief.

She sat down again on the bed, looking pleased and excited.

'And now tell me everything!'

I did not reply, but burst out laughing.

'Well really, Catherine, you are the limit! First you dispose of Bertrand, and once he's out of the way, you can't wait to hear something more exciting.'

'Don't make fun of me,' she said, in a "little girl" voice. 'Tell me all about it.'

'There's nothing to tell,' I replied shortly. 'I spent a fortnight on the Riviera with someone I liked. For various reasons the story ends there.'

'Is he married?' she asked slyly.

'No, a deaf-mute. Well, I must really unpack my suitcase.'

'I'll wait, you'll tell me in time,' she said.

The worst is that perhaps it's true, I thought as I opened my wardrobe, one day when I'm feeling depressed . . .

'Now about me,' Catherine went on, as if she were going to make a revelation, 'I'm in love.'

'With whom? Oh, the last one you told me about, I suppose.'

'If it doesn't interest you . . .'

But she continued her story all the same. I began to arrange my cupboard in a fury. Why did I have such idiotic friends? Luc wouldn't have put up with her for a moment. But what had Luc to do with it? This was my life after all.

'Well, I love him,' she ended.

'What do you mean by love?' I asked with curiosity.

'I don't know; loving, thinking about someone, going out with them. Isn't that it?'

'I can't say. Perhaps.'

I had finished putting everything away, and sat down on the bed, discouraged. Catherine made an effort to be nice.

'Dominique, you're crazy! You never think of anything yourself. Come out with us this evening. I'm going with Jean-Louis, of course, and one of his

friends, a very intelligent boy who goes in for litera-
ture. It will do you good.'

Anyhow, I did not want to telephone to Luc until
the next day. I was tired; my life seemed to be enveloped in a gloomy storm cloud, with Luc at times
in the centre as its only stable element. He alone
understood and helped me. I needed him.

Yes, I needed him. I could not ask him for anything
but, all the same, he was responsible for me in a way.
But I must not let him know it. Conventions must be
respected, particularly when defying them will injure
others.

'Very well,' I said, 'let's go and meet your Jean-
Bernard and his clever friend. I'm sick of intelligent
people – no, that's not true, but I only care for depressive intellectuals, the other kind get on my nerves.'

'The name is Jean-Louis, not Jean-Bernard,' she cor-
rected me. 'And what do you mean by the other kind?'

'The ones who can't appreciate that,' I said, point-
ing melodramatically to the window, and to the
bitter-sweet sadness of the lowering grey and pink
sky.

'All that's no good for you,' said Catherine uneasily;
and she held my arm to guide me as we went down
the stairs. She was a good friend after all. I couldn't
help liking her.

Her Jean-Louis was a good-looking, if rather shady
type, but not unpleasing. His friend Alain was far more
witty and amusing, with a sharpness to his intelligence,
a certain insincerity, and an ability to see other points
of view, all of which were lacking in Bertrand. We soon
left Catherine and her admirer, whose open display of
passion was rather out of place in a café. Alain took

me back to my pension, talking of Stendhal and litera-
ture in general. My interest was roused for the first
time for two years. He was neither handsome nor ugly,
quite nondescript. I was glad to accept his invitation
for lunch two days ahead, while hoping it would not
coincide with Luc's free day. Now my life was centred
round Luc, depended on him, and I had no choice but
to accept it.

13

I LOVED Luc, and this was brought home to me very forcibly the first time we spent a night together again. It was in a hotel facing a quayside. He was lying on his back after love-making, and talking with his eyes closed. He said: 'Kiss me,' and I raised myself on one elbow to kiss him. As I bent over him, I felt an absolute conviction that this man was the only thing that mattered in my life, and the knowledge made me quite dizzy. I realized that the almost unbearable pleasure of waiting to kiss him was the true meaning of love. I knew I loved him, and I lay down with my head on his shoulder without kissing him, with a little shiver of fear.

'You're sleepy,' he said, putting a hand on my back, and he laughed, 'you're like a little animal, after love you either go to sleep or feel thirsty.'

'I was thinking that I love you very much.'

'I too,' he said, and he pressed my shoulder. 'When we haven't met for three days why do you call me "vous"?'

'Because I respect you,' I said. 'I respect you and I love you.'

We laughed together.

'No, but seriously,' I continued, as if I had just had a brilliant idea, 'what would you do if I really loved you?'

'But you do really love me,' he said, closing his eyes once more.

'I mean, supposing I could not live without you, if I wanted you to myself all the time . . .?'

'I would be very worried,' he said, 'not even flattered.'

'And what would you say to me?'

I would say: 'Dominique, ah well ... Dominique, forgive me.'

I sighed. In any case his reaction was not the usual unpleasant one of the cautious, prudent kind of man, who says 'I warned you'.

'I forgive you in advance,' I said.

'Hand me a cigarette,' he said lazily. 'They are next to you.'

We smoked in silence. I said to myself: there it is. I love him. Probably this love is only an idea of mine and nothing else; but all the same, I see no way out of it.

Nothing else had existed for me during that whole week since Luc had asked me on the telephone: 'Will you be free the night of the fifteenth?' Every few hours I had thought of his words, remembering the casual tone of his voice, and each time I had felt a leap of joy which seemed to rise up and suffocate me. And now I was with him, and time was passing, slowly and inevitably.

'I'm afraid I shall have to go,' he said; 'it's a quarter to five already.'

'Yes,' I said. 'Is Françoise at home?'

'I told her I was going out with some Belgians to Montmartre. But the cabarets must be closing now.'

'What will she say? Five o'clock is rather late, even for Belgians.'

His eyes were still shut: 'I shall go in and say: "Oh those Belgians!" and stretch myself. She'll turn round and say: "The Alka-seltzer is in the bathroom," and go to sleep again. That's all.'

'I see, and tomorrow you'll make up a story about cabarets and Belgian morals, and so on?'

'Oh, it will just be a repetition. I can't be bothered with lies, or at least I have no time for them.'

'What have you time for?'

'Nothing at all. Neither time, nor strength, nor inclination. If I had been capable of anything at all, I would have loved you.'

'What difference would it have made?'

'None to us. At least I don't think so. Only I should have been unhappy on account of you, whereas now I'm happy.'

I wondered if this referred to what I had said earlier, but he put his hand on my head almost solemnly:

'I can say anything to you. I love that. I could never tell Françoise that I don't really love her, that there is no real and wonderful foundation to our relationship. At the root of it all is my weariness and my boredom. These are firm and solid bases in their way and one can build a lasting union on them. At least they remain unchanged.'

I lifted my head from his shoulder: 'They are . . .' I was about to add: 'nonsense,' because I wanted to protest, but I said nothing.

'What are they? Are you being childish?' he laughed tenderly. 'My poor darling, you are so young and defenceless, and fortunately so disarming, that I am reassured.'

He took me back to the pension. I was to lunch with him, Françoise, and a friend of theirs the next day. I kissed him goodbye through the car window. He looked old and tired, which touched me and for a moment made me love him more.

14

I AWOKE the next morning full of energy. Lack of sleep always agreed with me. I got out of bed, went to the window, inhaled the Paris air, and lit a cigarette, although I did not want one. Then I lay down again after glancing at myself in the mirror. I thought I looked rather interesting with my tired eyes. I decided to ask my landlady to heat the room the next day: 'It's icy cold in here!' I said aloud, and my voice sounded strange and husky. 'My dear Dominique,' I went on, 'you have a mania, you really must treat it: plenty of walks, careful reading, young people, perhaps a little light work . . .' I couldn't help being sorry for myself, but luckily I had a sense of humour. I was strong and healthy, why shouldn't I be in love? Besides, I was lunching with the object of my affections. So I went to Luc and Françoise, fortified by a physical well-being, the cause of which I knew.

I caught the bus with a flying leap, and the conductor, with the pretext of helping me up, took advantage of it to put an arm round my waist. I gave him my ticket and we exchanged an understanding smile such as may pass between a man and a woman on these occasions. I stayed on the platform holding the rail, while the bus went bumping along the street. I felt wonderful: I liked the sensation of tautness between my jaw and my solar plexus that I have after a sleepless night.

An unknown friend had already come when I arrived

at Françoise's. He was a fat, red-faced man with a dry manner. Luc was not there. Françoise told us he had spent the night in Montmartre with some Belgian clients, and had only got up at ten o'clock. Those Belgians were really a nuisance, they always wanted to go to Montmartre! I saw the fat man looking at me, and felt myself blush.

Luc came in looking tired.

'Hallo, Pierre, how are you?' he said.

'Weren't you expecting me?'

His manner was somewhat aggressive. Perhaps because Luc showed no surprise at my presence, but only at his.

'Of course I was, my dear fellow,' said Luc, with an exasperated little smile. 'Isn't there anything to drink here? What is that lovely yellow stuff in your glass, Dominique?'

'A neat whisky,' I answered; 'don't you recognize it any more?'

'No,' he said, sitting down on the edge of a chair, as one does in a station. Then he gave us all a glance, still like a traveller, absent-minded and indifferent. He had the air of a spoilt child. Françoise began to laugh:

'My poor Luc, you look almost as ill as Dominique. As for you, my dear girl, I'm going to put a stop to all this. I shall tell Bertrand to . . .'

She told us what she would say to Bertrand. I had not looked at Luc. Thank Heaven there was never any conspiracy between us regarding Françoise. It even had its funny side: we spoke of her between ourselves as of a very dear child who caused us a certain amount of worry.

'That sort of fun is no good for anyone,' said Pierre.

I suddenly realized that he knew about us, which explained his earlier look of contempt, his dry manner, and those half-allusions. Then I remembered that we had seen him in Cannes, and Luc had mentioned his being in love with Françoise. Now he was outraged, and was sure to tell Françoise. Like Catherine, he would want to hide nothing from his friends, do them a good turn, not abuse their hospitality. And if Françoise should find out and look at me with anger and contempt, and all those other feelings so unsuited to her, and, it seemed, so undeserved by me, then what would I do?

'Let's have lunch,' said Françoise; 'I'm starving.'

We walked to a nearby restaurant. Françoise took my arm, and the men followed.

'How mild it is,' she said, 'I adore the autumn.'

For some reason I was suddenly reminded of our room in Cannes, and Luc at the window saying: 'After you've had a bath and a good drink of whisky you'll feel better.' It was the first day, and I wasn't very happy; there were fourteen other days to come, fourteen days and nights with Luc. That was what I most desired at this very moment, and it would probably never happen again. If I had only known . . . but even if I had known, nothing would have been changed. Proust once wrote: 'It is very rare for happiness to be achieved at the exact moment it is desired.' It had happened to me that night: when I was with Luc, after longing for him all the week, my happiness was so intense that it made me quite ill. Perhaps this was due to the sudden ending of the emptiness that was my usual life. This emptiness had made me conscious that my life was cut in half, whereas the culmination of my happiness gave me the feeling that the divided halves and myself had at that moment joined together.

'Françoise,' called Pierre behind us. We turned round and exchanged partners. I found myself in front with Luc, walking in step along the red-paved avenue, and we must have had the same thought, for he gave me a questioning, almost a hard look.

'Well: yes,' I said.

He shrugged his shoulders resignedly, and raised his eyebrows. He took out a cigarette, lit it as he walked, and handed it to me. Each time something upset him this was his resource. And yet he was a man completely devoid of habits.

'That fellow knows about us,' he said.

He spoke pensively, and without obvious apprehension.

'Is it serious?'

'He's not likely to resist the possibility of consoling Françoise. But I don't think his consoling her will necessarily lead to much.'

I admired the self-confidence of the male.

'He's rather a silly ass,' he said, 'an old college friend of Françoise's. You know what I mean?'

I knew.

He added: 'I am worried because it will hurt Françoise. The fact that you are involved . . .'

'Of course,' I said.

'I would regret it for your sake if Françoise felt badly about the part you played. She could do you a lot of good, you know, and she's a friend you can depend on.'

'I have no dependable friend,' I said sadly. 'I have nothing I can depend on.'

'Unhappy?' he asked, and he took my hand.

I was moved by his gesture and the evident risk he was running. He was holding my hand as we walked together under Françoise's very eye, but then she knew it was only Luc, a tired man, who held my hand. Probably she thought that if he had a bad conscience he would not have done it. He was not taking much of a risk. He was a man who did not care about anything. I pressed his hand; here he was with me; I never ceased to be astonished that my days should be filled with the thought of him, and only him.

'I'm not sad,' I answered, 'not at all.'

I lied. I would have liked to tell him that I was unhappy and that I really needed him. But when I was with him, it all seemed unreal. For in truth there was nothing; there had been nothing but those fifteen enjoyable days, my reveries, and my regrets. Why then was I so tortured? That was love's painful mystery, I thought derisively. But in fact I was annoyed with myself, because I knew that I was strong enough, free enough, and gifted enough to have a happy love affair.

Lunch lasted a long time. I watched Luc anxiously. He was so handsome and intelligent and tired; I did not want to lose him. I made vague plans for the winter. As he left he told me he would ring me up. Françoise added that she too would telephone to arrange to take me somewhere to see someone.

I did not hear from either of them for ten days. I could hardly bear to think of Luc. At last he telephoned to say that Françoise knew everything and he would get in touch with me as soon as he could, but he was overwhelmed with work. His voice was gentle. I remained perfectly still in my room, unable fully to take it in. I was going to have dinner with Alain. He could do nothing for me. My world was in ruins.

I saw Luc twice during the next fortnight, once in the bar in the Quai Voltaire, and then in a room, where we found nothing to say to each other, either before or afterwards. Everything had turned to dust and ashes. I realized that I was not suited to be the gay paramour of a married man. I loved him. I should have thought of that sooner, or at least have taken it into consideration; the obsession that is love, the agony when it is not satisfied. I tried to laugh. He did not reply. He spoke sweetly and tenderly, as if he were about to die. Françoise had been very unhappy.

He asked me what I was doing with myself. I told him I was working and reading. I read with the object of telling him about the book I was reading, or went to the cinema to see a film he once told me had been directed by a friend of his. I sought desperately for bonds between us, something apart from the sordid pain we had inflicted on Françoise, but there was nothing, not even remorse. I could not say to him: 'Do you remember?' It would have seemed like cheating, and would have alarmed him. I could not tell him that I saw, or thought I saw his car everywhere in the streets, that I constantly began to dial his number and never completed it, that I feverishly questioned my landlady every time I came in, that everything centred upon him, and that I hated myself so much I wanted to die. I had no right to tell him any of these things, no right even to his face, his hands, his gentle voice, nor to any of the unbearable past . . . I was getting thinner.

Alain was kind, so one day I told him everything.

We were out for a long walk and he discussed my passion as if it were something in a book. This helped me to see it and speak of it objectively.

'You know perfectly well that it will end some time. In six months or a year you'll be able to joke about it.'

'I don't want to,' I said. 'It is not only a question of myself, it is all we were to each other; Cannes, our laughter, our understanding.'

'But that doesn't prevent your knowing that one day it won't matter any more.'

'I know it, but can't yet believe it. Anyhow, it is the present that matters, now, this very moment.'

We walked on and on. In the evening he came back with me as far as the pension and solemnly shook my hand. When I went in I asked the landlady if Monsieur Luc H. had telephoned. She said 'No' and smiled. I lay on my bed and thought of Cannes. I told myself: Luc doesn't love me; and it gave me a dull, sickly pain in my heart. I repeated it, and the pain came back more sharply. It seemed to me that I had made a discovery: from the fact that the pain was, so to speak, at my disposal and, armed to the teeth, was ready faithfully to answer my call, I could order it at will. I said: 'Luc doesn't love me,' and this astonishing thing happened. But even if I could turn the pain on and off as it suited me, I could not prevent it returning suddenly during a lecture or lunch, where it would attack and hurt me. I could do nothing about the misery of every day, my larva-like existence in the rain, feeling tired in the mornings, tedious lectures and conversations. I was suffering. I repeated the word to myself with curiosity, irony, anything that would cover up the sad evidence of an unhappy love.

What had to happen did happen. I met Luc again one evening. We drove through the Bois in his car. He told me he had to go to America for a month. I said 'how interesting,' then I suddenly realized: a whole month! I reached for a cigarette.

'When I get back, you'll have forgotten me,' he said.

'Why?' I asked.

'My poor darling, it would be better for you, so much better,' and he stopped the car.

I looked at his face. It was tense and sad. So he knew. He knew everything! He wasn't just a man one had to humour, he was also a friend. I clung to him all of a sudden. I laid my cheek against his. I stared out at the dark trees and I heard myself say the most incredible things:

'Luc, it mustn't happen. You can't leave me. I can't live without you. You must stay here. I'm so lonely, so dreadfully lonely, it is unbearable.'

I listened with surprise to my own voice. It was unashamed, youthful, supplicating. I told myself all the things Luc would say: 'There, there, you'll get over it, calm yourself,' but nevertheless I continued talking and Luc remained silent.

At last, as if to stop the flood of words, he took my head between his hands and gently kissed my mouth:

'My poor darling,' he said, 'my poor sweet!'

He spoke in a broken voice. I thought: 'so the time has come' and 'I'm really to be pitied,' and I began to cry against his waistcoat. Time was passing, and he would soon take me back to the house, exhausted. I would do nothing to stop him, and afterwards he would be gone. No! I couldn't allow it. 'No!' I said aloud.

I hung on to him. I would have liked to be him, to disappear.

'I'll telephone to you. I'll see you again before I leave,' he said. 'I'm so sorry, darling, so sorry. I was very happy with you. It will all pass, you know. Everything passes. I would give anything to . . .' He made a helpless gesture.

'To love me?' I said.

'Yes.'

His cheek was soft and warm with my tears. I was not going to see him for a month, he did not love me. How strange it was, this despair, and strange that one should ever recover from it. He took me back to the house. I had stopped crying. I was tired out. He telephoned the next day, and the one after. I had influenza the day he left. He came up for a moment to see me. Alain had just dropped in, and Luc kissed my cheek. He would write, he said.

15

SOMETIMES I woke in the night with a dry mouth, and before I had fully emerged from sleep something told me to lose myself once more in the warmth and unconsciousness which was my only refuge. But it was no use. I was already aware of my thirst and must get up and go to the wash-basin for a drink of water. When I saw my reflection in the glass by the dim light of the street lamp, and the tepid water was trickling down my throat, I was seized by a feeling of despair like a violent pain, and crept back to bed shivering. But I could not sleep, and the battle began. My memory and my imagination became two ferocious enemies. There was Luc's face, Cannes, what had been and what might have been, my body which needed sleep, and my mind which forbade it. I roused myself, sat up, and tried to reason it out: I loved Luc, who did not love me, therefore I was bound to suffer, and the only remedy was to break it off. I thought of ways of doing this: for instance, writing him a well-phrased, noble letter, explaining that all was over between us, but I found I was only interested in concocting a beautifully expressed letter that would be bound to bring Luc back to me. And no sooner did I imagine myself cruelly separated from him than I began to think about our reconciliation.

People always say one should control one's passions. But for whose sake should I do so? I was not interested in anyone else, nor in myself, except in so far as my relationship with Luc was affected.

I thought of Alain, Catherine, the streets, a boy who had kissed me at an impromptu party, whom I never wished to see again, the rain, the Sorbonne, cafés, maps of America (I hated America), my boredom; would it never end? It was more than a month since Luc had left. I had received one sad, tender little note from him that I knew by heart.

My one comfort was that my intellect, until then opposed to this passion, always mocking me and trying to make me feel ridiculous, leading me into violent arguments with myself, was gradually becoming more of an ally. I no longer said to myself: 'Let's put a stop to all this nonsense,' but 'How can I find a way out of my unhappiness?' Each night saw the same dreary repetition, but the days sometimes passed quickly, with lectures to occupy me. I tried to think of Luc and myself as if we were a 'case', but there were terrible moments when I stopped dead on the pavement with a feeling of rage and disgust. I would go into a café, slip twenty francs into the juke-box, and give myself five minutes' pleasure listening to the tune we had heard in Cannes. Alain began to hate it, but I knew every note. It reminded me of the scent of mimosa, and altogether gave me my money's worth. I did not like myself.

'Try to be calm, my dear!' said Alain, patient as ever.

I did not usually like being called 'my dear', but in this case it was rather a comfort.

'You are very kind,' I said.

'Not at all,' he would reply. 'I shall write my thesis on the subject of passion. It interests me.'

But the music finally convinced me that Luc was necessary to me. I knew very well that my need of him was both part of, and separated from, my love. I was still capable of disassociating in him the human being, the accessory, and the object of my passion: the enemy. The worst was not being able to despise him a little, as one usually does those who are only luke-warm towards one. There were also moments when I said to myself: 'Poor Luc, what a bore and a nuisance I would be to him!' and I reproached myself for not having taken our affair lightly, all the more as it might have attached him to me out of pique. But I knew very well he was incapable of such feelings. He wasn't an adversary, he was Luc. And so I went on and on.

One day, when I was just leaving my room at two o'clock to go to a lecture, I was called to the telephone. My heart no longer missed a beat as I answered it, because Luc was away. I heard Françoise's low, hesitating voice:

'Dominique?'

'Yes,' I answered.

There was absolute stillness on the staircase.

'Dominique, I meant to telephone to you before. Will you come and see me all the same?'

'Of course,' I said. I had my voice so much under control that it must have sounded quite artificial.

'Would you like to come this evening at six o'clock?'

'Very well.'

She hung up.

I was both upset and pleased to hear her voice. It brought back our week-ends, the car, lunches in restaurants, a whole way of life.

16

I DID not go to my lecture. I walked about the streets and wondered what she could have to say to me. Considering what I had already been through, it seemed to me that nothing could hurt me much. At six o'clock it was raining a little; the roads were damp and shiny under the lights, like the back of a seal. Coming into the house I saw myself in the looking-glass. I had grown very much thinner, and I vaguely hoped to fall dangerously ill and that Luc would come and sob at my bedside while I lay dying. My hair was wet and I looked hunted. I should appeal to Françoise's boundless kindness. I stayed a moment longer in front of the glass. Perhaps I should have tried to attach Françoise to me, plotted with Luc, and been more artful, but how could I do anything of the sort when my feelings were so deeply involved? I had been surprised at the force of my love and admired myself for it, but I had forgotten that it represented nothing for me except a chance to suffer.

Françoise opened the door with a half-smile, looking rather frightened. I took off my waterproof as I came in.

'Are you well?' I asked.

'Very well,' she said. 'Do sit down.'

She said 'vous'; I had forgotten that she used to call me 'tu'. I sat down. She looked at me, visibly amazed at my lamentable appearance, which made me feel sorry for myself.

'Will you have something to drink?'

'Yes, please.'

She fetched some whisky. I had forgotten the taste. I thought of my depressing room, the university restaurant, and the rust-coloured coat they had given me which had served me well. I felt strained and desperate, almost sure of myself, through my exasperation.

'Well, there we are!' I said.

I raised my eyes and looked at her. She was sitting on the divan opposite, staring fixedly at me; without a word. We might still talk of other things, and I could say to her on leaving, looking very embarrassed: 'I hope you are not too angry with me?' It depended on me; it would be sufficient to talk quickly before our silence became a double confession. But I was silent. The moment had come; I was living through it.

'I should have liked to telephone you sooner,' she said at last, 'because Luc asked me to, and also because I was sorry that you were alone in Paris, but . . .'

'I too ought to have rung you up,' I said.

'Why?'

I was going to say: 'to make my excuses', but the words seemed feeble. I began to tell the truth.

'Because I wanted to, because I felt very lonely, because I hated to think that you thought . . .'

I made a vague gesture.

'You look ill,' she said kindly.

'Yes,' I said resentfully. 'If it had been possible, I would have come to see you; you would have made me eat beefsteaks, I should have lain on your carpet, you would have comforted me. By ill-luck, you were the only person who could have helped me, and the only one I could not ask.'

I trembled, my hand shook. Françoise's gaze became

unbearable. She took the glass away, put it on the table, and sat down again.

'I was jealous,' she said quietly. 'I was physically jealous.'

I was dumbfounded. I expected anything but that.

'It was stupid,' she said. 'I knew quite well that you and Luc . . . it wasn't serious.'

When she saw my expression she made a gesture as though excusing herself, which seemed to me admirable.

'I mean,' she said, 'that physical infidelity is not really important; but I was always like that, and now still more, now that . . .'

She seemed to be suffering, and I was afraid of what she was going to say.

'Now that I am not so young,' she finished, and, turning her head away, 'less desirable.'

'No,' I said.

I protested. I had not thought this story could have another dimension, unknown to me, ordinary, sad, perhaps pitiable. I had believed it was my story; but I knew nothing of their life.

'It was not that,' I said, and got up.

I went towards her and remained standing. She turned round and smiled at me a little.

'My poor little Dominique,' she said. 'What a muddle.'

I sat down next to her and held my head in my hands. My ears were buzzing. I felt empty. I would have liked to cry.

'I like you very much,' she said. 'I don't like to think you have been unhappy. When I saw you the first time I thought we could give you a happier expression instead of that beaten look you had. It was not very successful.'

'I have been a little unhappy,' I said, 'but then Luc warned me.'

I would have liked to melt against her large, generous body, to tell her that I wished she had been my mother, that I was very unhappy; and to whimper. But now I could not even do that.

'He returns in ten days,' she said.

Did I still feel a shock? But Françoise must have Luc and her semi-happiness. I must sacrifice myself. This thought made me smile. It was the last effort to hide my unimportance. I had nothing to sacifice, no hope. I had only to put an end, or let time put an end, to an illness. This bitter resignation was not wholly devoid of optimism.

'Later, when it is all over, I hope to see you again, Françoise, and Luc too. Now there is nothing to do but wait.'

On the threshold she kissed me gently.

'Well, I shall see you soon.'

When I got home I fell on my bed. What had I said to her? What cold rubbish! Luc will come back. He will take me in his arms and kiss me. Even if he doesn't love me, he will be there, and this nightmare will be over.

After ten days Luc returned. I knew it because I passed his house in a bus the day of his arrival, and saw his car. I went back to the pension and waited for his telephone call. It did not come. Neither that day, nor the next, and I remained in bed to wait for it, pretending I had influenza.

He was there and he had not rung me up. After a

month and a half's absence! My shivering, half-hysterical laughter and obsessive apathy all added up to one thing – despair. I had never suffered so much. I said to myself: this is the last blow, and the hardest!

The third day I got up and went to my lectures. Alain walked with me again. I listened attentively to all he said. I laughed. Without knowing why, I was haunted by a certain phrase:

'Something is rotten in the state of Denmark!'

I kept repeating it.

The fifteenth day I woke to hear music in the courtyard coming from a kind neighbour's radio. It was a beautiful Andante by Mozart, as always evoking the dawn, death, and a certain way of smiling. I listened to it for some time, motionless in my bed. I felt rather happy.

The landlady called me. I was wanted on the telephone. I put on my dressing-gown without hurrying and went downstairs. I thought it must be Luc, and that it was no longer very important.

'How are you?'

I heard his voice. It was his voice, but whence came that feeling of calm, of peace? Something in me had changed. He asked me to have a drink with him the following day. 'Yes, yes,' I said.

I went up to my room very thoughtfully. The music had ceased, and I regretted having missed the end. I was surprised to see myself smile in the glass. I did not stop myself smiling, I could not. Once more, I knew it, I was alone. I wanted to repeat that word to myself: alone, alone. But what of it? I was a woman, and I had loved a man. It was a simple story; there was nothing to make a fuss about.